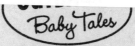

Newborns, new arrivals, newlyweds…

In a beautiful but isolated landscape, three sisters follow three very different routes to parenthood against all odds and find love with brooding men….

Discover the soft side of these rugged cattlemen as they win over three feisty women and a handful of adorable babies!

MICHELLE DOUGLAS

The Cattleman,
the Baby and Me

OUTBACK
Baby Tales

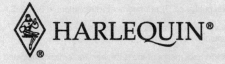

HARLEQUIN®

TORONTO • NEW YORK • LONDON
AMSTERDAM • PARIS • SYDNEY • HAMBURG
STOCKHOLM • ATHENS • TOKYO • MILAN • MADRID
PRAGUE • WARSAW • BUDAPEST • AUCKLAND

Recycling programs
for this product may
not exist in your area.

ISBN-13: 978-0-373-17658-8

THE CATTLEMAN, THE BABY AND ME

First North American Publication 2010.

This edition published by arrangement with Harlequin Books S.A.

For questions and comments about the quality of this book please contact us at Customer_eCare@Harlequin.ca.

www.eHarlequin.com

Printed in U.S.A.

At the age of eight, **Michelle Douglas** was asked what she wanted to be when she grew up. She answered, "A writer." Years later she read an article about romance writing and thought, *Ooh, that'll be fun.* She was right. When she's not writing she can usually be found with her nose buried in a book. She is currently enrolled in an English master's program for the sole purpose of indulging her reading and writing habits further. She lives in a leafy suburb of Newcastle, on Australia's east coast, with her own romantic hero—her husband Greg, who is the inspiration behind all her happy endings. Michelle would love you to visit her at her Web site, www.michelle-douglas.com.

To Mum, with love.

CHAPTER ONE

'THAT'S the Jarndirri out station down there.'

At the pilot's words Sapphie Thomas turned from the baby sleeping beside her to stare out of the mail plane's window. Anna and Lea Curran—her best friends—had grown up on Jarndirri. Sapphie had spent a lot of time there herself. She'd deftly fed that piece of information to Sid, the pilot, earlier. Sapphie didn't get into small planes with strange men without them knowing she had friends in high places—friends who could come to her aid in a flash if the need arose.

She stared down at the out station and longing and pain hit her in equal measure. Her chest tightened. 'You're not going to land, are you?'

Her chest tightened even more. She didn't want Sid to land. She didn't want to step foot on Jarndirri at the moment. For lots of reasons—not least being the letter she'd received two days ago.

She pushed that thought away. She didn't have time to dwell on it. Instead, she thought how a landing might wake Harry, and she didn't want that. Her twelve-month old nephew, it seemed, hated flying. He hated landings and take-offs. He hated the dust and the heat and the flies. He hated the glare of the sun in its cloudless sky, and hated Sapphie trying to change his nappy in the close confines of the plane.

He hated it all—with a capital H—and he had the lungs to prove it. Sapphie had wanted to wail right alongside him.

She'd wanted to wail because Harry hated her too.

During the long, hot five hours they'd so far endured on the plane he'd only stopped crying when she'd given him his bottle—most of the contents of which he had then thrown up all over her shirt. Finally, through sheer exhaustion, he'd fallen asleep. She didn't want him woken for any reason whatsoever. So *not* landing at Jarndirri would suit her perfectly. She waited for Sid's answer.

'Nah,' Sid drawled. 'They radioed through earlier. They don't have anything for me to collect. And as I don't have anything for them...'

Sapphie gulped back a sigh of relief. In the next instant her shoulders went all tight again. 'What about the main Jarndirri station? Will you be landing there?' The Jarndirri homestead was several hundred kilometres northeast of the out station, but that didn't mean it wasn't on Sid's mail route.

Don't be an idiot, she chided herself. You're not going to accidentally bump into Anna or Lea out here. Neither was currently in residence at Jarndirri. Anna was in Broome with Jared, and Lea was at Yurraji—the property in the far north that her grandfather had left her.

And Bryce had died six years ago. She wasn't going to run into him.

The plane bounced as it hit a pocket of turbulence. Sapphie's stomach churned and bile rose up to burn her throat. Normally she was a good flyer.

Normally? Ha! Normally she wouldn't be flying over the northwestern corner of the Australian continent—one of the most remote regions in the world—without any form of invitation. And if she did it would be to see Anna or Lea, not to track down some man she'd never met in her life before.

There was nothing *normal* about the turn her life had taken in the last two days.

'The main Jarndirri station is on a different mail run,' Sid said. 'Mail delivery to this part of the Kimberley's on a Thursday. Mail delivery to *that* part of the Kimberley's on a Tuesday.'

Sapphie closed her eyes for a moment, beyond grateful that she'd arrived in Broome yesterday. If she'd left it another day then she would have had to wait an entire week to catch the mail plane to Newarra. Broome was small. Anna would have heard that Sapphie was in town, and...

And that didn't bear thinking about.

Beside her, Harry stirred. Sapphie held her breath. When he didn't wake, she let it out in one long, slow exhalation. Please, please, please let him sleep for a bit.

He needed the rest.

He needed the peace.

And she needed to think.

What a mess! She'd have dropped her face to her hands, only she didn't want Sid to see how desperate she was.

'You're looking a bit peaky,' he said anyway.

She had a feeling that as far as descriptions went 'peaky' was being kind. She wrestled for a smile. Sid had been kind. 'Perhaps because I'm *feeling* kind of peaky.'

He jerked his head in Harry's direction. 'Hardly surprising.'

A surge of protectiveness washed over her. Harry might hate her, but she'd fallen in love with him from the first moment she'd clapped eyes on him. 'He's not a good flyer,' she murmured.

'Lots of kiddies aren't.'

'I'm sorry, Sid. This must have been the flight from hell for you, and—'

'There's nothing to apologise for,' the pilot said gruffly.

Yes, there was. There was a wealth of things to apologise for.

Sapphie's eyes burned. She closed her hand gently around Harry's foot. How could she make up to him for everything that had happened? How could she help him feel loved and secure again? There weren't enough apologies in the world to make up for the fact that Harry had been lumped with her instead of someone who would know what to do, who would know how to comfort him properly and ease his fears… someone who deserved the right to look after him. That person wasn't her.

There was no one else.

'Oh, Harry,' she whispered, bending over him and pushing the sweat-soaked hair from his forehead. 'I'm sorry.'

She'd found out about Harry's existence two days ago, when her nineteen-year-old sister, Emmy, had been arrested on drug charges. Two days ago… The day Sapphie had turned twenty-five. The same day she'd discovered Bryce Curran was her biological father.

She pressed the heels of her hands to her eyes. She'd spent the last three years searching high and low for Emmy. With no success. When Emmy had rung two days ago Sapphie had thought it the best birthday present she'd ever received.

But her little sister hadn't rung to wish her a happy birthday. She hadn't even remembered it *was* Sapphie's birthday. She'd rung from Perth Central Police Station—'*I need help.*' When Sapphie had arrived, Emmy had pushed Harry into her arms with a fierce, 'Promise me you'll find his father.'

Sapphie had promised. What else could she do? Somehow she'd let her little sister down in every way that counted. She would not fail her on this. She *would* find Harry's father.

She knew what it was like to grow up without a father, always wondering who he was, never knowing his identity. She would not let that happen to Harry.

Unbidden, a ripple of relief speared through her. There was someone other than her who could take responsibility for Harry, and she thanked God for it. Emmy had given her dates, locations…and a name. 'Liam Stapleton—a cattleman in the

Kimberley. You're familiar with the area. Anna and Lea Curran will help you if you ask them.'

Sapphie had to wrestle with the bile that rose through her. She couldn't ask them. Not now. Not knowing what she knew. If Anna and Lea ever discovered that Bryce had been unfaithful to their dying mother…and that Sapphie was the result of that infidelity…

'You going to be sick?'

Sapphie started, pulled in a breath and shook her head. She fought to find another smile. And won. 'No, I'm just a bit worn out, that's all.'

'Why don't you get some shut-eye like that littlie of yours? Do you the world of good.'

Littlie of hers? She swallowed back the hysteria that threatened to swamp her. She didn't have the energy to correct him. If she'd made a different decision seven years ago she might have a littlie now, but…

She shied away from the thought. She couldn't follow it. Not today. Not for as long as she was responsible for Harry.

A weight slammed down on her so hard she half expected the plane to lose altitude. She gazed at Harry and a lump lodged in her throat. At eighteen she'd lacked her little sister's courage. *I'm sorry, Harry. I wish there was someone better to step up to the plate for you. I wish…*

'It'll be another forty minutes before we reach Newarra.'

Newarra—Liam Stapleton's cattle station. Sapphie closed her eyes. 'Thanks, Sid, a catnap might be just the thing.' She had to save her energy. She'd need it all once they landed if she was to fulfil the promise she'd made to Emmy—to see that this Liam Stapleton accepted responsibility for his son.

A wave of exhaustion hit her. It would be no easy task. Not when Liam Stapleton was as ignorant of Harry's existence as Sapphie had been two days ago.

* * *

'You did say Liam was expecting you, like—right?'

'That's right.' Sapphie kept her eyes closed in case they betrayed her lie.

'Looks like he's waiting for you.'

Her eyes flew open. They were flying over Newarra right now? She pressed her face to the window and took in the golden-green grasses and low scrub below, a stand of boab trees and the glint of a river in the distance. An enormous homestead emerged beneath them, the cool white of its weatherboards and the greenness of its surrounding gardens crisp and inviting in the harsh sunlight.

And then the airstrip came into view. Waiting to one side was a white four-wheel drive ute. The air left her lungs on a whoosh. Emmy hadn't lied. It appeared that Harry's father was in charge of a cattle dynasty that rivalled Jarndirri's in size and scope.

The plane descended. She stared at the white ute and her stomach started to churn. She hadn't rung Liam Stapleton. She hadn't sent a telegram or an e-mail or anything. She hadn't wanted to give him a chance to surround himself with lawyers, to fob her off—to fob Harry off.

The plane touched down and she fought back the panic scratching at her throat. Staring down at a sleeping Harry, she squared her shoulders. She was doing the right thing. Harry belonged with his father. After his initial shock, Liam Stapleton would see that too. He *would* do the right thing by Harry. She'd make sure of it.

Sid jumped out of the plane the moment he brought it to a halt. Sapphie glanced at Harry, who'd remained sleeping. She bit her lip and then glanced back outside. She wouldn't be far away. If Harry woke, she'd hear him. Filling her lungs with air, she scrambled out of the plane after Sid.

'G'day, Liam,' Sid drawled.

'Sid.'

Sid hitched his head in Sapphie's direction. 'Got your

visitors here in one piece.' He rubbed one ear. 'Not sure about meself, mind.'

A pair of the most startling eyes Sapphie had ever seen swung around to survey her. Blue. Bright blue. 'Wasn't expecting visitors, Sid,' he drawled. All the same he pushed away from the ute towards her.

Sapphie forced herself forward, hand outstretched, though for the life of her she couldn't seem to find a smile. 'My name is Sapphire Thomas, Mr Stapleton.'

Long, lean, work-roughened fingers closed about her hand. He was so big! She stared up into his face. She had to throw her head back to do so—he stood at least six feet two inches. It was a hard face, grim and lean, tanned, but it didn't frighten her. Just for a moment she let the relief trickle through. If he'd frightened her she'd have had to climb back on board the plane and fly back to Broome and leave all this up to lawyers. She always followed her instincts.

Always.

'Should I know you?'

The dry, rough drawl skittered along the surface of her skin and for a moment she thought it might raise gooseflesh. She let out a breath when it didn't. 'Not exactly.'

'Mind telling me what you're doing here?'

It almost made her smile. Kimberley cattlemen—they didn't waste their words.

And then, just like that, it suddenly struck her. She'd spent the last two days thinking Liam Stapleton would try and duck out of his responsibilities and reject Harry, but the longer she stared up into this man's face the more convinced she became that he would do no such thing.

He pushed the brim of his hat further back, as if to give her a better opportunity to study his face.

A face like that—grim and stern—it could do with some joy.

A child was a joy.

A child was a gift.

'Well?' he drawled.

The worry and stress of the last two days all suddenly seemed worth it. A smile broke through her. 'Mr Stapleton, I've brought you your son.'

Liam planted his hands on his hips, told himself to breathe deeply. 'Did you just say *son?*' He uttered the words with cutting precision.

The ridiculous smile that lit up Sapphire Thomas's face started to slip. 'That's…that's right.'

He hadn't left Newarra in nearly two years. He hadn't been with a woman at all during that time. He'd never met this woman in his life. He'd have remembered if he had. He folded his arms, raised an eyebrow. 'And how old is this particular son of mine?'

Anyone who knew him would know from the tone of his voice that now was the time to back off. Sapphire Thomas didn't.

'Twelve months,' she said, without so much as a blink of her eyes.

Anger, swift and hard, punched through him. With the effort of long practice he reined it in. 'Ms Thomas, I do not have a son.' His ex-wife had made sure of that.

'But—'

'No buts!'

He let some of the anger from the black pit of his heart reach out to touch her. Her eyes widened. She swallowed and took a step back. *Good.*

'So you can haul yourself back on that plane and return to wherever it is you come from.'

Her mouth opened and closed. 'But—'

Liam turned away, told himself he didn't care. He would not be the fall guy for a desperate woman ever again.

'Twenty-one months ago at the Perth agricultural show you met my sister—Emerald Thomas.'

Her words rang clearly in the still air. They sounded

formal, with the same tone a judge would use when casting sentence. They sounded rehearsed, as if she'd gone over and over what she was going to say countless times. His lips twisted. They sounded fake.

'You spent a week together at a resort on Rottnest Island.'

Against his will, he spun around. Rottnest Island! His heart pounded loud in his chest.

The Thomas woman raised an eyebrow. The gesture seemed somehow wrong in the white pallor of her face. Her eyes flashed green, and it occurred to him *she* should be called Emerald, not her sister.

If there was a sister.

'Rottnest Island,' she repeated. 'Ring any bells?'

Yes, damn it. His hands clenched. But…

A baby's screams suddenly and abruptly split the air. Sapphire Thomas swung away to dive inside the plane in instant response. She emerged a moment later with a baby capsule cradled in her arms. He found his anger again. Lies! These were all lies, and cruel ones at that.

One thing was clear—this child was not his. This woman could take this baby, get on the plane, and slink back into whatever hole she'd crawled out of. He would not let her take advantage of his family's grief.

'Hey!' he shot at her when she lifted the child from the capsule. 'I told you to get back on that plane.' He stabbed a finger at her. 'You can take your baby and get back on that plane, because there's no way—'

The baby turned to stare at him.

'No way that—'

The baby's face crumpled. It leaned so far away from him it was in danger of falling right out of the woman's arms.

But that baby. It…

She balanced the baby on her hip and half turned, shielding him from Liam with her body. 'Don't you go scaring him, you big, horrible *bully*.'

Liam couldn't move. All he could do was stare. At the baby. A baby who was the spitting image of Liam at the same age…of Lachlan…

A baby who was the spitting image of Lucas!

The resemblance had to be a coincidence. He hadn't fathered this child. But…

What about Lachlan or Lucas?

His stomach turned. No, not Lucas. Lucas had been dead for…

She'd said twenty-one months ago.

Lucas had been alive twenty-one months ago. And able-bodied. He hadn't yet had the accident that had crippled him.

Twenty-one months ago Lucas had still been able to walk, ride…and presumably make love. Not that Liam had kept track of his trysts. But…

She'd said Rottnest Island, and—

His hands clenched. Anyone who knew his family, anyone who'd known Lucas, could spin a story like this.

But when he stared at the child it didn't feel like a story.

She backed up a step and a shudder rocked through her. 'What kind of man are you?' she whispered.

He barely heard her. Lucas had gone to Perth for the ag show. He'd stayed at Rottnest Island—Liam had the postcard to prove it. This child…could he be Lucas's son?

A lump tried to lodge in his throat, but he forced it back, refused to allow it to fully form.

Sapphire Thomas speared him with those amazing green eyes. 'Look, let's get one thing clear. I am not letting you abandon Harry—got it?' She lifted her chin. 'We can deal with this like adults or we can leave it to the lawyers. It's your call.'

He shifted his gaze from the child to her. She didn't look like a liar or a cheat, but then neither had his ex-wife.

It would be better to let the lawyers deal with it.

Under his continued scrutiny she turned a shade paler, and

then she reached up and fastened the top button on her oversized and decidedly rumpled shirt.

He blinked.

'And you can stop looking at me like that,' she said, in a voice so acid it would dissolve the rust from weathered corrugated iron. 'I haven't slept in two days. I've been stuck in that shoebox of a plane for over six hours. I've been weed on, vomited on, it's as hot as blazes, and the dust is driving me mad! If I look like a bag lady, then—'

'You don't look like a bag lady.' He didn't know what had possessed him to say that. Only she *didn't* look like a bag lady. And if she was feeling the heat, why wasn't she undoing a few buttons or taking that long-sleeved shirt off instead? Even with the baby cradled in her arms he could make out the lines of the T-shirt she wore beneath it.

She continued to stare at him. Her chin didn't drop. As a ploy to force him to confront her claim, it worked. Her sister and his brother? He tried to weigh it, assess it.

Why hadn't she said Lucas was the father, then?

His gut clenched. The day darkened. Given all he'd found out about Lucas after the accident, it made an uncanny kind of sense. It could all still be a pack of lies, of course, and Sapphire Thomas might still be a liar and a cheat. Or her sister might have taken advantage of her and spun her a whole pack of lies. Those things were just as possible.

Something hard and heavy settled in his gut. He averted his eyes from the child. Regardless of how much he wanted to, he could not dismiss this woman's claims. They warranted investigation. He owed Lucas that much.

And much, much more.

One thing was clear, though. He had to disabuse this woman of the misapprehension she was currently labouring under. 'Ms Thomas, I know when I said this before that you didn't believe me, but I am not that child's father.'

'But—'

'I have never met your sister, and I have never been to Rottnest Island. I certainly haven't taken a holiday—not there, not anywhere—in the last five years.'

Her green eyes darkened in confusion. 'But—'

'He ain't either,' Sid piped in. 'It's become a bit of a joke in these parts.'

Liam had no reason to lie. If he had a son, he would never turn his back on him. His hands clenched. Never!

All the blood drained from Sapphire's face. Liam pushed his more sombre thoughts aside and braced himself to move forward and steady her if she started to sway. From somewhere, though, she found the strength to stiffen her spine and lift her chin. The lines of exhaustion that fanned out from her eyes tugged at him.

'But Emmy named you. She… She said…' She swallowed, obviously trying to come to terms with his revelation. Bruised eyes met his. She recoiled from him as if he'd threatened to strike her…or worse. 'You'd deny your own son?'

'No!' The word broke from him, harsher than he'd meant it to. 'I wish—'

He couldn't finish that sentence. 'I'm not his father.' He dragged in a breath. 'But I think I know who might be.'

Her jaw dropped. He took advantage of her momentary silence to cast a sidelong glance at Sid, and hoped that she'd interpret it correctly—he didn't want to discuss this any further in front of the other man.

Her eyes narrowed. 'Do you? Or is this just a way of putting me off?'

'I'm not trying to brush you off, Ms Thomas. You're right—we do have a lot to discuss.' He glanced at the sky. The afternoon was lengthening. 'Where are you staying?' It wouldn't do to let this sit. He wanted to get to the bottom of it as soon as possible.

'Oh, I…' She blinked, as if she hadn't expected him to be so reasonable. 'I'm staying at the Beach View Motel in Broome.'

'Not tonight, you ain't,' Sid said unceremoniously, shuffling forward. 'I'm having a lay-over in Kununurra. You didn't say this was a return trip. You just said you wanted a ride to Newarra,' he added, when Sapphie's jaw dropped.

'But—'

'I'm not heading back to Broome for another two days.' Sid glanced at Liam, grimaced. 'And the yearling sales are on.'

Which meant every available room in Kununurra would be booked out. Liam bit back something rude and succinct. He didn't want a woman at Newarra. He didn't want a child there either—reminding him, taunting him, plaguing him with all that he'd lost. Not even for two days.

'There's nothing for it.' Sid clapped Liam on the back. 'You're going to have to put Ms Thomas and her baby up.'

If the woman hadn't been standing within hearing distance he'd have let fly, told Sid exactly what he thought of that plan. His lip curled. Sid was trying to protect his bachelor pad in Kununurra, that was what. A makeshift bachelor pad in an airplane hangar, Liam reminded himself. It was no place for a woman or a child. And he could hardly blame Sid for that when it was exactly what he was doing too. Trying to do.

He reminded himself of all he owed Lucas.

'What's he talking about?' the Thomas woman snapped.

Liam planted his hands on his hips. 'You're going to have to stay here tonight.'

She stiffened. 'I don't think so. I'll book into a motel or a B&B in Kununurra.'

'Ms Thomas, with the yearling sales on you won't get a room in Kununurra.' He swept out an arm to indicate the emptiness of the landscape. 'It's not like we're exactly teaming with other options out here, you know?' Kununurra was nearly four hundred kilometres away. Broome was closer to six hundred. Newarra's nearest neighbour was a three-hundred-and-fifty kilometre drive. He bit back his impatience. 'You don't have any other choice.'

She backed up a step. 'A woman always has a choice.'

Her words came out low and vehement. She reminded him of a spooked heifer. He pursed his lips, adjusted his hat. He worked at keeping his voice low and easy. 'I guess you could camp out if you wanted. I could lend you some gear.' He lifted a deliberately casual shoulder. 'But my housekeeper would have my hide if I let you do any such thing.'

There was no chance he was letting her camp out on his land. Who knew what trouble she'd get herself into? But long practice told him it would be better for Sapphire Thomas to come to the conclusion about the best course of action in her own time. Women were like that—contrary. High-maintenance. Trouble.

'Beattie's cookin' is a real treat too,' Sid added.

As Liam had hoped, her shoulders relaxed at the mention of his housekeeper. He forced himself to glance at the child nestled in her arms. 'And there is the child to consider.'

She blinked. Her tongue snaked out to moisten her lips—a gesture that betrayed her nervousness. Then her chin shot up and Liam had to own she hid those nerves pretty well. Against his will, something akin to admiration warmed his veins.

'Harry,' she shot back like a challenge. 'His name is Harry.'

The warmth fled. His throat went dry as sawdust. 'Harry,' he forced himself to say, 'might prefer a cot to a tent.'

She chewed her bottom lip.

'Of course there's also the added bonus of hot water and electricity up at the homestead.'

He could see her almost salivate at the mention of hot water. She shifted her weight from one leg to the other. 'I'll need to make a couple of phone calls.'

'We have a satellite phone. You're welcome to use it.'

Finally, she lifted one shoulder. 'I suppose if there's no chance of getting a room in Kununurra…'

'No chance at all,' Sid said cheerfully. He touched her arm, then tried unsuccessfully to chuck Harry under the chin. 'Liam's a good man. You'll be okay here.'

She swallowed and nodded. She met Liam's eyes. 'Then thank you. That's very kind of you.'

'Not kind. Necessary,' he shot back, disturbed by the flash of vulnerability he'd sensed in her. 'We have a lot to discuss.'

CHAPTER TWO

'I WON'T let you down, Harry,' Sapphie whispered against Harry's hair, her arms tightening around him as she watched Liam and Sid unload her and Harry's things from the plane. For the first time in two days Harry didn't try to push away from her.

He must be exhausted. And scared.

She rummaged through their bags until she found Horsie—a stuffed toy from her own childhood, and the only toy she'd had in her house to give to Harry. She held him up for Harry to see. Harry didn't smile even when she pressed the toy's face lightly to his cheek and made loud smoochy kissing noises, but he did wrap one arm tightly about Horsie's neck. Then he stared up at Sapphie with eyes so wide she couldn't help it. She had to drop a kiss to his brow.

'I promise you,' she whispered again. 'I won't let you down.' When Sid left, Liam would tell her who Harry's father was, and then she could start her search anew.

She turned. Liam had carried all their bags to his car in one go. If there was a spare ounce of flesh on the man, she couldn't see it. He wore a long sleeved khaki workshirt tucked into his jeans, and although she could make out the breadth of his shoulders all the honed muscle beneath was hidden. She knew it would be honed.

He was so…big! Tall…broad…strong. A woman wouldn't stand a chance if he…

An icy prickle crawled across her scalp. She grabbed hold of the panic before it could spiral free. There was a housekeeper at the homestead. She wouldn't be alone with this man.

Besides, instinct told her he wasn't the kind of man who would take advantage of a woman's vulnerability. She paid close attention to her instincts. He might be as unforgiving and elemental as the land he worked, and she'd be crazy to underestimate him—only a fool would cross him—but, like the land, he lacked deliberate malice. She stared at the rugged angles of his face. He had a savage grandeur that was grim and beautiful at the same time, like the amazing landscape of the Kimberley region.

Still…a woman could never be too careful. She would ring Anna this evening.

'Whenever you're ready, Ms Thomas.'

Sapphie blinked at the dry drawl before heat invaded her cheeks. How long had she been staring at him? Her hand flew to her top button. A sigh juddered out of her when she found it firmly done up.

'Sapphie,' she said. 'Please call me Sapphie.' And then, 'Do you know the Currans of Jarndirri?'

He swiped his brow with his forearm, then shrugged. 'I've met Jared West a few times. I knew Bryce Curran.'

Yeah, well, he was my father. She didn't say the words out loud. Still, it wouldn't hurt to let him know she had connections out here. 'My mother used to work at Jarndirri as a station cook during muster. Anna and Lea Curran are my dearest friends in the world. We went to school together.' She added a lie for good measure. 'Anna's expecting us for dinner this evening. That's why I need to use your phone—to let her know where we are. So she won't worry.'

At first he didn't say anything, and, while his eyes might be the most amazing blue she'd ever seen, it didn't mean she could read them. And then, 'You're trying to tell me you're not a stranger out here?'

That was exactly what she was telling him. 'You needn't worry I'll wander off and get myself lost. And I do know the difference between a King Brown and a Taipan.' She had a healthy respect for snakes—especially those two varieties.

'That's good to know.'

His eyes held a hint of…something. Amusement? Was he laughing at her? Not that she minded if he was—amusement was something she could deal with. Besides, a smile would soften the line of his mouth. A laugh might well transform his face entirely.

Not that his amusement, if that was what it was, manifested itself into anything as outwardly betraying as a smile. It was becoming all too apparent that Liam Stapleton was a self-contained man. She wondered what it would take to smash through those barriers and unleash the man within.

She shivered at the thought. It wasn't something she was ever likely to find out.

Not that she wanted to. She was here for Harry. That was all. She'd find out who Harry's father was, and then she would leave again. Simple.

Funny, but it didn't feel simple as she lowered Harry to his capsule.

Harry started to cry. He held onto Horsie tight and snuffled his face against the toy's softness. It shocked her how that action pierced straight to her womb. Tears burned the backs of her eyes. She blinked them away. 'Shh, Harry, it's all right.'

Only they both knew it wasn't. His mother was facing a three-year jail sentence, and his father was… Who *was* his father? Exhaustion swamped her, the sun beat down, and she could feel herself start to sway.

Liam moved forward, touched her arm. 'Let's get you both up to the homestead. You can freshen up and then we can talk.'

She nodded, then gestured to the capsule and Harry. 'I'm sorry, but I'm going to have to sit in the back with him.'

'Do whatever you need to do. We're only a couple of kilo-metres from the homestead, so it's not going to take long.'

The big cattle and sheep stations in the Outback placed their airstrips several kilometres from their homesteads as a fire precaution. She slid onto the back seat beside Harry with a grateful sigh. She was glad they didn't have too far to go. She wasn't sure she was up for much more travel-ling today.

Liam paused in the act of closing her door, another frown in his eyes. 'When did you last eat?'

Food! Sapphie's eyes lit up and her mouth started to water. 'Ooh, ages and ages ago. Harry and I, we'd kill for a Vegemite sandwich—wouldn't we, Harry?'

Harry didn't smile, but he bobbed his head up and down in imitation of Sapphie.

A minor victory!

Unbelievably, Liam laughed.

A major victory! Sapphie tried not to gape. It made him look younger—a lot younger—and milder, in the same way the cliffs and valleys in the Kimberley ranges lost all their hard edges at twilight.

'I'm sure we can rustle you up a couple of Vegemite sand-wiches,' he said before closing her door.

Sapphie did her best to catch her breath. She tried to convince herself it was the heat and dust that made it hard to breathe.

As she'd seen from the plane, the Newarra homestead was big...grand. The coolness of the white weatherboard was welcoming. The broad grandeur of the six wide stone steps that led up to the double front door hinted at a stability she had never experienced, of a home lovingly crafted to provide more than just shelter for its occupants. The shadiness of the deep verandas with their simple wooden balustrades beckoned.

A sigh whispered out of her. Everything about the home-stead, even down to the rose garden, was designed to refresh and please the eye. The height of summer was long gone, but Sapphie could imagine the cool promise of the homestead shimmering in the heat of a midday sun, when temperatures soared in excess of forty degrees and dark clouds gathered op-pressive on the horizon.

A square of lush green lawn surrounded it all. Bore water, Sapphie guessed, because no farmer out here would waste precious water resources on a lawn and garden.

Unless he had a wife and it meant a great deal to her. And he loved her very much.

Sapphie glanced at Liam. He brought the ute to a halt at the edge of the lawn. He didn't drive around to the collection of buildings behind the homestead. She glanced back at his home. Did he have a wife?

He'd only mentioned a housekeeper. When she turned back, she found him watching her in the rearview mirror. 'Your home is beautiful.'

'It's been in the family for generations.'

'Do you have any family living with you at the moment?'

'Getting nervous?'

It sounded like a taunt. She lifted her chin. 'Just wonder-ing what to expect, that's all.'

He pushed out of the car, turned back and leant down to say, 'It's a bit late for those kinds of considerations, don't you think?' and then closed the door.

Sapphie unbuckled Harry's capsule and climbed out too, met Liam's eyes across the roof of the car. 'It's never too late to take other people's feelings into consideration.'

He stilled, but with the sun in her face, and the brim of his hat shading his, she couldn't see his expression let alone try and decipher it.

Before he could make any answer, an older woman—in her fifties, Sapphie guessed—came bustling out from the house. 'Did my wools arrive?' She pulled up short when she saw Sapphie.

'Beattie, this is Sapphie Thomas and Harry.' He glanced at Sapphie, but not at Harry. 'They've come to stay…for a bit.'

Sapphie gulped. *For a bit.* She hadn't thought how long this might take. As usual she'd leapt into action without thinking it through properly. But whenever she stopped to think things through—big things—she froze. Like she was doing now with Anna and Lea. She couldn't afford to freeze where Harry was concerned.

She glanced down at him and he lifted his arms to her. Perhaps surrounded by strangers he now saw her as his only ally. 'Oh, Harry,' she whispered. How could she tell him he was putting his faith in the wrong person? She wanted to weep for him.

She lifted him out, cuddled him close.

Liam gestured. 'This is Mrs Beatson—the housekeeper here at Newarra.'

She pasted on a bright smile when the older woman started across the lawn. 'It's nice to meet you, Mrs Beatson.'

'Call me Beattie, my dear, everyone does. Mrs Beatson was my mother, God rest her. It's lovely to have visitors.' Her eyes lit up when they landed on Harry. 'Ooh, and you've brought a littlie—what fun!'

But as she reached out a hand to Harry he threw his face into Sapphie's neck with a cry. Sapphie wanted to apologise, but she didn't get a chance. With a sympathetic *tsk-tsk*, Mrs Beatson murmured, 'Poor little tyke. He's all worn out.' And she promptly set about abusing Liam for keeping Harry and Sapphie standing in the sun for so long.

Sapphie only had time to grab the bag containing Harry's essentials before Mrs Beatson had taken her arm and was propelling her up the path towards the house. 'Oh, but shouldn't we help unload the car?'

'Nonsense, dear, it's what men have muscles for.'

That made Sapphie grin. All the same, she turned back to glance at Liam.

'Beattie will show you to your room.' His lips twisted. 'Take your time. I'm not going anywhere. I'll be in the living room when you're ready.'

With a quiet nod, she turned and followed the housekeeper.

She let out a sigh of pure pleasure when they crossed the threshold. 'Oh, Mrs Beatson—Beattie.' She corrected herself at the housekeeper's frown. 'What a lovely home.'

Dark waxed floorboards and antique furniture greeted them, the dim shade a distinct relief after the glare of the sun outside. An overriding sense of peace and calm stole over her. It was ridiculous, she knew, but it felt as if nothing bad could happen in such a lovely place.

'It's so…big!'

'It is at that.' Beattie chuckled.

Sapphie swallowed as she followed the housekeeper into the kitchen—state of the art. Beattie set a kettle on to boil.

Sapphie moistened her lips. 'It's way too big for one person. Does Liam live here all by himself?'

'He does at the moment, dear.' Beattie turned pensive. 'This is the family home, mind, so the rest of the family all have rooms here, but they haven't visited in a while. At Christmas it can get quite rowdy, but…well, not last Christmas.'

Before Sapphie could ask why, Beattie beckoned to a door off to the left.

'Those are my rooms down there if you need to find me. Now, let's get you and this little man here settled.'

She led Sapphie down a long corridor—more waxed floorboards, softened by a Persian carpet runner in burgundy. She threw open a door at the end to reveal a beautifully appointed room with moulded cornices and French doors leading out to the shade of the veranda.

'And here's the attached nursery,' Beattie said, leading her through an adjoining doorway.

'Oh!' Sapphie turned on the spot. Everything she and Harry could possibly want, even down to an antique wooden rocking horse, was here. 'It's lovely.'

Beattie gave a satisfied sigh. 'This nursery has seen four generations of Stapleton children. Liam and Belinda had it redecorated.'

'Umm... Belinda?'

Beattie shook her head. 'Sorry, dear, I'm prattling on, aren't I? We haven't had visitors in an age and I've forgotten how to act.' Her voice lowered a notch. 'Belinda was Liam's wife. They divorced a few years back. He's a good man. He didn't deserve that.' She stared at Harry and her smile broadened again. 'Oh, my, but it warms the heart to have a child in the house again, let me tell you. And don't you worry, dear. Nobody will disturb you down this end of the house. Liam hasn't visited these rooms since—'

She broke off. Sapphie had to bite her tongue to stop from asking Since when?

'You'll have to excuse an old woman's ramblings.'

'There's nothing to excuse,' Sapphie said with a determined smile and a shake of her head.

'Now, the bathroom is just down the hall. And don't hesitate to ask if you need anything.'

'Thank you.'

Beattie disappeared, leaving Sapphie and Harry alone. And it suddenly occurred to Sapphie that not only was Liam not Harry's father, but he no longer had a wife either, which meant he was a single man.

Her mouth went dry. She eyed the phone on the bedside table, bit her lip. She didn't want to talk to Anna—not yet, not after everything she'd just found out. But for safety's sake someone needed to know where she and Harry were.

She hauled in a breath and forced herself to pick up the receiver. As long as she didn't have to look Anna in the eye, she should be able to lie convincingly enough. If Anna sensed that something was wrong, Sapphie could simply say she was worried about Harry and Emmy. Which was the truth. In part.

Sapphie bathed Harry and dressed him in clean clothes. He didn't exactly co-operate, but he didn't fight her either.

She tried telling herself it was an improvement, a step forward for little Harry. Common sense told her he was just too tired at the moment to kick up a fuss.

She had to find his father. She had to find someone who could look after him properly and give him everything he needed. She had to remove herself from his world before he started to rely on her…before she tainted him too. She wasn't the kind of woman who should be trusted with the care of a child.

A lump lodged in her throat as she stared at him. He was so little. He was such an innocent. And he didn't deserve any of this! Longing welled through her. She did what she could to banish it.

With a gulp, she kicked herself back into action—showered in double-quick time, pulled on clean clothes, and then towel-dried her hair, tugged a comb through it. Neat, tidy, clean—that was all the occasion called for.

She started towards Harry, who lay in the middle of the queen-sized bed. She pulled up short, bit her lip, cast a glance at the door. Not the smallest spark of sexual interest had lightened Liam's eyes when they'd rested on her. Not at the airstrip. Not in the car. And she'd like to keep it that way.

She pulled a cotton sweater from her suitcase, tugged it on over her head. She adjusted the long sleeves, fastened the three buttons at the collar. Jared, via Anna, had told her Liam was a good man. Beattie and Sid had both said the same thing. It was what her instincts told her too. She prayed that none of them had been deceived.

* * *

Liam shot to his feet the moment he realised Sapphie hovered in the doorway. He wasn't sure what had alerted him to her presence. Her fragrance, perhaps? She smelt of peaches.

'Come in.'

She took a few hesitant steps into the living room. Her hair was damp, as if she'd just showered. Perhaps she used peach-scented shampoo?

She wore a clean pair of jeans and a shirt that had to be at least three sizes too big. She balanced Harry on one hip and clutched a baby bottle full of milk in her other hand. With a piece of terry cloth in the most vivid orange tossed over her shoulder she shouldn't look sexy.

She didn't!

He pushed the thought right out of his head as soon as he was aware of thinking it. He didn't give two hoots what Sapphie Thomas looked like.

He gritted his teeth. He didn't need a woman like this at Newarra. He didn't need *any* woman. He forced himself to focus on the bright cloth and nothing else.

She reached up a hand to finger it. 'Do you know they make nappies in the most amazing range of colours now? I like them loads more than the plain old white ones, don't you?'

He didn't know what to say. A nappy was a nappy, as far as he was concerned. 'You need to change him?'

She shook her head. 'This—' she pulled the nappy from her shoulder and glanced around the room at its vast array of sofas and armchairs '—is to save your furniture.'

'It's survived generations of children. No doubt it'll survive generations more.'

'Yeah, but only through the hard work of women like Beattie. If I can save her any work, then I will.'

For some reason that made him want to smile. 'She'd think it a small price to pay for having a child in the house again, believe me.' He glanced at Harry, and any desire he had to smile fled. He didn't need a child at Newarra either. 'You didn't want to put him down for a nap?'

Her gaze darted away. 'He's unsettled. I wanted to keep an eye on him.'

He took a step towards her, noted the dark circles under her eyes and remembered how she'd said she hadn't slept in two days. Suddenly he wished she could have all the sleep she needed. He could go and work on that new brumby for a couple of hours, as he'd planned before she'd turned up on his doorstep...or rather airstrip. They could talk once she was rested.

He opened his mouth, but she got in first. 'May I take a seat?'

He deliberately hardened his heart, warned himself against going soft...especially where a woman was concerned. He and Sapphie Thomas had too much to sort out. He had too much to find out.

'Of course...please.' He motioned her further into the room and pointed to a sofa. 'That one is particularly comfortable.' And, from his armchair, it would afford him a good view of her face.

He watched her settle Harry back against the cushions, the orange nappy arranged around him. Liam kept his eyes on Sapphie's face. It was easier than looking at Harry. His jaw tightened. The furniture at the Newarra homestead might survive several more generations of children, but none of those children would be his.

Some of the tension seeped out of him, though, as he continued to watch Sapphie. She was easy on the eye. She might not be conventionally beautiful—her mouth was too wide and her jaw too square—but her features were mobile and constantly changing, a play of light and shadow. Though perhaps there was more shadow than light at the moment. He frowned.

If she was aware of his scrutiny she gave no sign of it. Oversized sweater, buttons fastened again. She was telling him in no uncertain terms—*hands off*.

His lips tightened. That suited him fine. She didn't need to tell him twice.

She showed Harry his bottle…smiled and talked nonsense… sighed when he didn't respond. Harry took his bottle, though, rolling onto his side and suckling eagerly. Which reminded Liam…

'Beattie made us a pot of tea and some Vegemite sandwiches.' He lifted the plate of sandwiches towards her.

'Ooh, yum!' She seized one and bit into it. 'You'll have to excuse me, because I mean to eat this with more gusto than grace,' she said, mouth half full.

He'd have smiled, but as he watched her devour half a sandwich and then reach for another his heart started to burn. 'When did you last eat?'

'Last night.'

He leapt up. 'That's not—'

He broke off when she put a finger to her lips and gestured to Harry. The child's eyes were closed. In repose, Harry's face lost its wariness. Liam's heart burned harder. Part of him wanted to reach out and touch the child—make sure he was real. The greater part of him shied away.

Sapphie's voice hauled him back. 'When I found out the mail plane was doing its run today I didn't have time for breakfast. And, while I grabbed plenty of supplies for the trip, both Harry and I felt a bit queasy on the plane.'

Liam opened his mouth, but she'd pre-empted his next question. 'And, yes, we both drank plenty of water. Neither one of us is dehydrated.'

He sank back into his chair. Then slid forward to pour the tea. If she hadn't eaten since last night… 'How do you take your tea?'

'White and two, thanks.'

He handed her a cup, and then watched in fascination as she swallowed it down in three swigs. Beattie had used the good china—the cups were tiny. He poured her a second cup as she finished the rest of her sandwich. He held out the plate towards her again.

She took the cup with a murmured, 'Thank you,' but declined another sandwich. He set the plate back to the coffee table, aware of a vague sense of disappointment—it had given him a certain satisfaction to feed her.

She took a measured sip of her tea, eyeing him over its rim, and then straightened as if refusing to surrender to the sofa's beckoning softness. She set the cup on the coffee table. 'Liam, who do you think is Harry's father?'

She didn't want to make small talk, and he didn't blame her. They didn't have anything small to talk about. Harry might be small in stature, but not in any other sense of the word. She wanted answers.

Who *did* he suspect was Harry's father? He dragged a hand down his face. Lucas, that was who. He bit back an oath. *What a mess!*

He stared back at her, tried to keep his voice measured, his breathing even. 'I suspect that the child there is my nephew.'

CHAPTER THREE

SAPPHIE stared at him—nephew? He thought Harry was his *nephew*? She didn't know whether to laugh in relief that her search hadn't taken her too wide of the mark or not. One look at Liam's face and she decided not to. She bit her lip. From what Beatttie had said none of Liam's family was currently in residence at Newarra, but surely a simple phone call would solve everything?

And then Harry would have his daddy.

She pressed her hands to her heart, willing it to slow, and slumped back against the sofa's softness. 'What is your brother's name?'

'Lucas.' The word scratched out of him, barely audible. He cleared his throat. 'Lucas,' he said again, this time louder.

'Lucas?' she whispered, remembering the betrayal that had stained Emmy's eyes when she'd said, 'He promised to come back for me.' 'Why do you think he's Harry's father?'

Liam started to rise, then stopped, as if he thought any sudden movement might startle her. 'Can I show you the family album?'

He was treating her the same way Bryce had treated a frightened colt. She didn't mind. It suited her purposes perfectly for the moment. She didn't want Liam taking her assent about anything for granted.

At her nod, he strode across the room to a bookcase. He

was just a little too lean and broad and hard for a woman's peace of mind. It would suit her just fine if he kept his distance.

He came back, laid a heavy photo album across her knee and retreated to his chair. She opened the first page and just stared. She turned to the second page…went back to the first page…turned to the third. And it suddenly fell into place— why Liam had broken off mid-tirade and stopped threatening to throw her back on the mail plane. The faces of the babies staring out at her from the album were identical to that of the baby sleeping beside her.

'Harry is…'

'The very image of me and my brothers,' Liam confirmed, his lips twisting.

She stared at him, willing him to show just a little bit of joy at discovering he had a nephew. She understood that he might still be wrestling with the magnitude of the surprise, but…

She swallowed and shook herself. 'Who's this? And this?'

Liam leant across the arm of the sofa. He touched one brown finger to a photograph. 'This is me… That's my brother Lachlan, my sister Lacey… And this here is Lucas.'

Until around the ages of three, the photographs of Liam, Lachlan and Lucas seemed identical. They still looked like brothers after that, but their individual differences started coming to the fore. Not just physically either. In every photograph of him after the age of five Liam stood with his back ramrod-straight, staring intently at the camera. Lachlan, with a grin full of mischief, was usually showing off. And Lucas, when he wasn't laughing, had a tendency to duck his head— a little uncertain, a little shy.

They were gorgeous kids. And they had all grown into seriously gorgeous men.

As Sapphie turned the pages of the photo album, a picture formed of a close-knit family bound by love and laughter and mutual respect. Longing yawned through her. She'd spent her whole life wanting to belong to a family like this.

She glanced down at Harry. Could all this history and heritage be his?

Finally she handed the album back to Liam, and thankfully he moved away, back to his armchair, where his heat and his scent couldn't beat at her. He smelt of horse and leather and native grass—scents she associated with the Kimberley and with good times. For as long as he'd sat so close she'd had to fight the urge to lean into him. She swallowed and told herself to stop being so fanciful.

'The resemblance is remarkable.'

'Yes.'

If the photos were any indication, Lucas laughed a lot. He looked as if he'd make a wonderful father—full of fun and laughter...and love. The opposite of the man sitting across from her.

Her instincts told her Liam was a good man, but nobody could accuse him of being a barrel of laughs, could they? The lines around his eyes and mouth grew more pronounced. She wished he'd smile. She should have known the moment she'd clapped eyes on him that Emmy wouldn't mess with a man like Liam. He wasn't the kind of man one messed about with.

'You should probably have a look at this.'

He held something out to her. A postcard. She couldn't decipher the emotion that momentarily twisted his features, but an icy premonition suddenly seized hold of her. She didn't want to read that postcard. She knew that with every atom of her being. She forced her nerveless fingers to take it. A postcard from Rottnest Island. She turned it over. It was signed by Lucas. The date was twenty-one months ago. She frowned. It seemed innocuous enough.

Liam held up two sheets of paper. 'This is Lucas's credit card statement from twenty-one months ago. Multiple transactions were made at a resort on Rottnest Island. It appears he was there for about a week.'

Just as Emmy had said. But…

She stared at Liam, at the credit card statement he held, and her mouth suddenly went dry. 'Liam, where is Lucas?'

He stared back at her with eyes as dark as tar. 'Lucas is dead. He died eight months ago.'

All the strength drained from Sapphie's arms and legs. She stared at his white-lipped face. 'I'm so sorry,' she whispered.

He gave a curt nod.

She found it hard to bear witness to such naked grief. She knew Liam would resent the fact that she'd seen it, and would reject any attempt at comfort she made, so she turned to stare at Harry. Her throat went tight and her eyes burned

Poor Harry!

No! She refused to believe it.

'The resemblance—it could be a coincidence! It doesn't mean—'

'We'll have a DNA test done to make sure. It'll put every-one's minds at rest.'

'But if Lucas was Harry's father…' She let the sentence trail off because she couldn't bear to finish it.

'They'll be able to tell from my DNA how closely related I am to Harry.'

'No! It doesn't make sense.' She had to find Harry's father. *She had to!*

'Emmy said *you* were Harry's father, not Lucas. Why would she say that if…?'

He rested his head in his hands, suddenly looking as old as the ranges on the horizon.

Her fingers curled into her palms. 'What?' she whispered.

'Lucas had me on a bit of a pedestal.' The word ground out of him as if he loathed it. 'He was only twenty-three when he died—fourteen years my junior. Our mother always called him her happy accident.'

A mother who had lost her son. For a moment Sapphie could barely see Liam through the sheen of her tears. She gulped them back.

'After his accident, when we were at the hospital, I did hear that when Lucas went out on the town he'd sometimes introduce himself as me.'

She stared. 'But why?'

He lifted one shoulder. 'I never asked him. At the time there were more important things to worry about.' He scowled, dragged his fingers back through his hair. 'At the time I figured he was play-acting at being the manager of Newarra—it was what he wanted more than anything. If it's any consolation, I don't think he deliberately set out to deceive your sister.'

'But it still doesn't mean he's Harry's father! This could all be a mistake.'

'For the last four years Lucas was the family's representative at the Perth Agricultural Show. He was definitely on Rottnest Island at the time you claim Harry was conceived.'

'But—'

'I know this isn't the scenario you were expecting, or hoping for, but taken all together the facts tell their own story.'

All she could do was stare at him—this man who spoke such hard, unrelenting words. A tremble ran through her. Her fingers started to shake, and then her hands, her arms, her shoulders—she couldn't stop them. The postcard fluttered to the floor. Harry's father was dead.

No!

She stared at Liam and shook her head. 'No,' she whispered. Harry's father was supposed to step forward and claim him, love him.

'I'm sorry, Sapphie.'

Her shaking grew so violent she thought it might shake her bones from her skin. She'd failed Emmy. She'd failed Harry. She'd change places with Lucas in an instant if...

She dropped her head to her knees and let the shaking overtake her. Liam leapt to his feet, but she held up a hand to ward him off. With a muttered oath, he fell back into his chair.

Finally, when the trembling had subsided, she lifted her head. 'I'm sorry.'

'You're exhausted!'

His words came out harsh, almost angry. She didn't blame him. She and Harry being here had raked up the most painful memories for him.

They were both silent for a moment. Liam finally roused himself. 'Is Harry an orphan?'

It took her a moment to realise what he was asking. She stiffened. 'No!'

'Then where is his mother? Why isn't she here with the child?'

She wasn't quite ready to tell him that. 'She's…indisposed at the moment.'

He surveyed her for a long moment. 'What does she want? Why are you here, Sapphie?'

Sapphie's mouth went dry. She wanted to pick Harry up and cuddle him close. 'Emmy wanted Harry's father to take over full custody of him.' But that was an impossible dream now.

Liam's head shot up. 'Why?'

The single word reverberated around the room. That wasn't a question she was prepared to answer yet either, so she just shook her head.

Liam shot to his feet. 'I need to water the horses.' The words left him abrupt and hard. 'I'll see you at dinner.' He started for the door.

'Liam?'

He stopped. Turned.

She swallowed at the grim cast of his mouth. 'What happened to Lucas?'

His face shuttered closed. 'He died.' Without another word he disappeared through the door at the far end of the room.

Sapphie closed her eyes. She opened them a moment later to stare down at the child sleeping beside her. Nausea rose through her. She'd just run out of options for this innocent child and there was nothing she could do about it. She pressed a hand to her mouth. *Oh, Harry, I'm so sorry.*

Sapphie surged out of bed and into the nursery the moment Harry's wails broke through the sleep fog of her brain.

'Oh, Harry!'

She picked him up and tried to cuddle him, but he wouldn't let her. Any momentary sense of connection or trust he'd felt towards her earlier was gone.

She bounced him in her arms, rubbed his back and tried to soothe him, but he refused to be soothed. 'Did you have a nightmare, beautiful boy?'

She had to gulp then because his waking, daytime world must seem the real nightmare to him—missing his mum, in the care of a virtual stranger, with any routine he'd had tossed out of the proverbial window.

She changed his nappy—no easy feat when he kept trying to twist away. Especially when she was no expert at nappy-changing. She checked his temperature, checked him over for rashes...for anything that might be causing him pain or discomfort.

She came up with a blank. Just as she had last night. Just as she had the night before that.

He could be teething...

She glanced at the clock—eleven p.m.

She tried playing silly games with Horsie to distract him, singing nursery rhymes, walking to and fro with him in her arms and rubbing his back.

He screamed through all of it.

Finally Sapphie sat him in the middle of the queen-sized

bed and dragged her hands through her hair. *Think!* She didn't know what to do. She didn't know how to help him, how to comfort him. A mother would know what to do.

She swung away to wring her hands. She didn't deserve to be a mother. She'd known that for the last seven years. If there were anyone else...

How did she make amends for what she'd done?

It suddenly hit her. That was exactly what she was trying to do now. She hadn't done right by her own child, the child she'd aborted, but she'd make sure she did right by Emmy's. It wasn't enough, it would never be enough, but it was something.

She stared at Harry. His cheeks were hot and red with crying, misery and bewilderment were leaking down his face, and her throat thickened. *She* deserved all this. But Harry—he didn't!

Food. The thought slammed into her and her back straightened. He'd had a bottle this evening, but he hadn't kept much else down throughout the rest of the day. Could that be it? 'Are you hungry, Harry?'

She picked him up and raced down the hallway to the kitchen. She heated his bottle. She grabbed a tin of chocolate custard.

He refused both.

She even tried giving him his bottle on the same sofa he'd curled up on earlier in the day, hoping it would hold some familiarity or positive association for him.

Nothing doing.

Fighting back tears of her own, she walked him up and down the length of the living room. 'Oh, Harry, Auntie Sapphie *wishes* she could make things right for you. She'd do anything to make it right for you.'

He kept right on crying. His screams tore at her. If she were a different kind of person, a better person, he wouldn't have to go through this. She was inadequate, pathetic, worse than useless—all she could do was stay awake and bear witness to his distress.

'What's wrong with him?'

The voice from the doorway didn't even make her jump, which was testament to her exhaustion and her growing sense of desperation. But when she cast a glance back over her shoulder her host's bulk, outlined by the light of the lamp, made her swallow. She automatically checked the neckline of her shirt.

Stop it! She didn't own anything with a plunging neckline. This shirt, teamed with a pair of baggy tracksuit pants, could hardly be called beguiling in anyone's language.

'Is he ill?'

'I don't think so.' She couldn't keep the tremor out of her voice. 'He doesn't have a temperature or a rash or…or anything that I can see.'

Liam took a step into the room, then another. He shoved his hands into the back pockets of his jeans. He obviously hadn't gone to bed yet.

'How long has he been crying?'

'What time is it?'

'Just gone midnight.'

She stifled a sigh. 'About an hour.'

'An hour!' Liam jerked and stiffened to his full height. It made her aware of just how tall he was…how broad. 'Something must be wrong with him.' He started for the door at the far end of the room. 'I'll radio the flying doctor service.'

'No.' Sapphie shook her head. It felt unutterably heavy on her shoulders.

He swung back. 'But an *hour*. It's—'

'It's nothing. We did this for four hours last night. Then we had a three-hour break before doing it all over again for another two hours.'

He stared at her, visibly appalled. 'But… Have you tried giving him his bottle?'

Frustration hit her, low and hard. 'What do you think?' she all but growled. 'I've tried everything!' She held Harry out towards him. 'You want to give it a go?'

Liam backed up, raised his hands. 'He doesn't know me. I'll frighten him.'

'So? He's only known *me* for two days!'

As if to prove Liam's point, Harry screamed louder. Sapphie pulled him back in close. 'Oh, Harry, Auntie Sapphie's sorry. She didn't mean to scare you.'

Harry did his best to twist away from her. She swallowed down a lump. It bruised her throat and lodged as a dead weight in her chest. He didn't want her touching him. He knew what she was. What further proof did she need that as a mother substitute she was the worst?

She tried to fight the blackness that threatened to descend around her, the tears that clogged her throat. And then, amazingly, Liam moved forward and lifted Harry from her arms. And suddenly she could breathe again.

Harry didn't stop crying, but his sobs no longer tore at her chest or rang so loudly in her ears. She fell into the nearest chair—Liam's armchair—and just stared at man and child.

Liam didn't know what to do with the squirming, screaming bundle he held. It was just he hadn't been able to bear the look on Sapphie's face any longer. She'd looked as if she'd been about to break. And if she'd had to deal with this for *six hours* last night…

He couldn't regret trying to ease her burden, but now that he'd taken the child he didn't know what to do with it. He glanced at her. Maybe she'd give him a hint?

She smiled. He marvelled that, given her exhaustion and her concern for the child—not to mention how upset she'd been earlier to learn of Lucas's death—she'd found the strength for even the smallest of smiles.

'Your arms are going to get dreadfully tired, holding Harry like that,' she observed.

His arms were held out at a straight ninety-degrees from the rest of his body. Harry dangled at their ends, securely clamped beneath his armpits. Gingerly, Liam pulled the child in close against his chest. Harry didn't stop crying. As he had with Sapphie, he tried to twist away. For something so small, he sure had some strength in that little body of his.

Don't drop him!

Liam promptly sat. In the very middle of the sofa. Shored up by the plump softness of cushions on all sides.

He tried jiggling Harry on his knee. Harry would have none of it. The volume of his cries had tension coiling tight in Liam's stomach and knotted his shoulders. Sapphie had done this for *six hours* last night? He'd held his nephew for less than two minutes and—

Don't panic. You're a grown man. Harry is just a baby and—

Just a baby? He had to clamp down on the harsh laugh that threatened to burst from him. Five years ago he'd have done anything for a baby, and now here he was holding one in his arms—admittedly it was his nephew, not his son—and he didn't have a clue what to do.

As if she sensed his growing sense of inadequacy, Sapphie slid off her seat, collected a soft toy from the floor and knelt down in front of him and Harry.

'Hey, Harry,' she crooned, prancing the toy from one end of the sofa to the other, dancing it across Harry's feet and Liam's legs along the way. It seemed strangely intimate, though he knew she hadn't meant it to be. 'Horsie hates to see you so sad.'

Harry didn't stop crying, but he did stop squirming. And then he leant forward and seized the stuffed horse and buried his face in it. Liam's gut twisted and turned. Poor little kid. He was tired and out of sorts, and Liam didn't know how, but he wanted to make things better for him.

'It gets under your skin, doesn't it?' Sapphie whispered.

As his nephew's warm weight filtered into his conscious-ness, Liam found he couldn't speak. All he could do was nod.

Sapphie gulped, her eyes suspiciously bright. 'Okay, so far we've tried his toys, his bottle, and walking up and down. We've changed his nappy, changed his clothes. We've tried cuddles, silly faces, silly voices…chocolate custard. If there's anything else you can think of…?'

Liam went to drag a hand down his face and then thought better of it, kept it anchored around Harry instead. 'Have you tried singing to him?'

'I tried nursery rhymes.'

She pressed the heels of her hands to her eyes, and for a moment Liam was tempted to haul her up onto the sofa beside him and order her to rest.

'Oh, Harry…' She pulled her hands away. 'You know what your Grandma Dana used to do when I was sad?'

Harry barely paused for breath between wails. Liam hadn't known a baby could cry for so long without pause.

'Your Grandma Dana, she'd sing ABBA songs to me and your mum.'

At the word ABBA, Harry stopped mid-wail. Sapphie's jaw dropped. Liam straightened. He stared down at Harry. Harry's face screwed up again. 'Sing an ABBA song,' Liam ordered.

Sapphie launched into a seriously off-key rendition of 'Mamma Mia'. Harry stopped crying. Just like that. Liam couldn't believe it. And with the cessation of the crying came an easing of the tension in that little body. Harry didn't rest back against Liam, but he did stop fighting him.

An ache gripped Liam's gut and split open a canyon of longing.

The song came to an end. Harry didn't start crying again. Sapphie stared at Harry, then at Liam with wide, excited eyes, and then she smiled—really smiled. Like the smile she'd sent him when she'd climbed out of the mail plane, the smile that had accompanied her words: *'Mr Stapleton, I've brought you your son.'*

But Harry *wasn't* his son.

That ache gripped him with greater purchase. A fierce protectiveness seized hold of him…and other emotions beat at him—emotions he had no hope of deciphering for as long as the scent of talcum powder, warm milk and soft baby invaded his senses.

'Ooh, Harry, you know what?'

Like Harry, Liam focussed on Sapphie. It was easier than trying to deal with the confusion raging through him. The scent of peaches reached out and soothed him.

She touched Harry's knee. He didn't recoil. 'Your Grandma Dana taught your mum and me this special dance. Your mum loved it, and I bet you know it!'

She leapt to her feet. 'You so much as laugh…' she shot at Liam out of the corner of her mouth.

'I wouldn't dream of it. I swear.' He meant it too. This woman—she deserved a medal.

She started to hum the introduction to another song. Liam's gut clenched when Harry's eyes went wide. And then she launched into the most bizarre song-and-dance routine Liam had ever seen. It involved a combination of the Twist and the Stomp, with a grand finale that included the Mash-Potato. It was a fifties-inspired, bouncy piece of nonsense, and Harry loved it. His eyes went even wider, and when he started clapping Liam wanted to clap too.

When the song came to an end, she dropped to her knees in front of them, breathless. Liam found his own breath suddenly hard to catch too. She clapped her hands and beamed at Harry. 'Ooh, that was a bit of fun, wasn't it?'

Harry clapped his hands some more. He stared at her for what seemed like a lifetime, then leant forward and placed one plump hand against her cheek. And then he smiled.

'Oh!' She sank back on her heels as if her leg muscles had dissolved beneath her. Her eyes filled with tears, and that ache gripped Liam all the fiercer.

He wanted Harry to smile at *him* like that!

'Do you think I should sing that again?' she asked.

Lines of exhaustion fanned out from her eyes. He shook his head. 'Rest, Sapphie.'

'But what if he starts crying again?'

Liam settled back against the sofa. And then he opened his mouth and started to sing—'Fernando'.

Sapphie's jaw dropped, but only for the briefest moment. She showed Harry his bottle and he took it. She brushed the baby curls from his face and whispered, 'Auntie Sapphie loves you.' Then she eased back to rest against the armchair opposite, curling her arms on the seat and resting her head on them.

As if to imitate her, Harry leant back against Liam's chest, nestled into him and closed his eyes. Liam's heart expanded to fill the hole left inside him five years ago. A hole he'd spent the last five years trying to ignore.

Belinda's inability to fall pregnant had devastated him. He'd tried to hide it. He'd tried telling himself that it was the events that had occurred afterwards that had really torn his heart out. But he wondered now if that were true. Was it Belinda's betrayal that had hurt him? Or the fact that he'd been denied a child—children—of his own?

CHAPTER FOUR

LIAM slammed to a halt at the edge of the vegetable patch, stopped in his tracks by the sight of Sapphie pegging out washing. Strands of purple and green reached out to flick his arm from a nearby plumbago bush. Bees hummed and the sun shone down with cordial abandon.

He recognised the shirt she'd worn when she'd arrived yesterday, moving gently on the line to the same rhythm as the plumbago. The shirt she'd said had been weed on and thrown up on. It had definitely showed evidence of both. Yesterday.

But it wasn't the sight of her newly washed shirt and jeans, but the tiny shorts and T-shirts pegged up beside them—ludicrously tiny—that brought him up short, that twisted his gut with such an unexpected cramp of longing he had to clench his hands and lock his knees to stay upright. And the nappies, those crazily coloured nappies, that flapped in the breeze, taunted him with all he didn't have.

Sapphie bent down to the washing basket and then straightened, her hair flashing gold and chestnut in the sun. He blinked. She was pegging out one of his workshirts!

The world tilted. He gritted his teeth and forced it to right itself again, to set itself in the straight lines he'd fixed for it five years ago. It might all *look* like a picture of domestic bliss, but he knew it for what it was—an illusion. And he refused to be seduced by it.

He dragged a hand down his face. In all fairness, Sapphie Thomas wasn't trying to manipulate him. She might be struggling, but she hadn't asked him for anything.

It was clear she'd been landed with her sister's child out of the blue. Two days. That was how long she'd said she'd known Harry. There was a story there, but he suspected she wasn't ready to tell him what it was. There was no denying, however, that she was doing her best for Harry...and probably for her sister as well. He'd be struggling in her shoes too.

A grin hit him. They should be blue suede shoes. That ridiculous dance of hers last night. She'd thrown herself into it with her whole heart. And in return she'd won Harry's heart.

That ache of his started up with renewed vengeance, and the knowledge that had been building in him ever since he'd held his nephew's warm weight in his arms last night burst through him now.

He wanted Harry as a part of his life. He wanted to plug the gaping hole left by Belinda's betrayal. Liam's hands clenched.

He owed it to Lucas. He owed it to his entire family. Harry would heal more than just his heart. The blood pounded at his temples. Harry could help him make amends.

He and Sapphie had to talk!

'Hello, there.'

He started, and found her staring at him, the now empty washing basket clasped against one hip. She must be on her way back to the house.

She fingered her top button. 'Hiding in the bushes?'

'I was...uh...admiring the view.'

She blinked. He smothered a curse and waved to the clothesline.

She turned and then laughed. 'Doesn't it look wonderful?'

Bright orange, lime-green, cobalt blue and hot purple nappies flapped like pennants.

'Very festive,' she pronounced, turning back.

He forced himself forward—out of the bushes, so to speak. 'It took me by…surprise.'

He didn't know what he'd said that was so funny, but her lips started to twitch. 'You're back early. Beattie said we wouldn't see you till lunchtime.'

'I wanted to check that you and Harry were okay.'

'Absolutely! We slept like logs when we finally made it to bed. Did us the world of good too. We slept in till eight o'clock!'

He found one corner of his mouth momentarily breaking free from its usual confines and hooking upwards. 'Scandalous,' he teased.

'Hey, I know what hours you guys keep out here. You and Beattie would've been up at five or five-thirty.'

'Yeah, but we're getting ready for muster.' *She* didn't need to keep those hours.

'Muster?' Her eyes danced. 'What fun.'

The other corner of his mouth kicked up too. Muster was the busiest time of year. It was a logistical nightmare, chaotic, and at times dangerous. And, like most cattlemen, he loved it. Her grin told him she knew it too.

It struck him then that Sapphie looked at home out here. More at home than Belinda had ever done. He rolled his shoulders, shoved his hands in his pockets. If Sapphie had spent time at Jarndirri then that would explain it.

'Liam, about last night?'

'Yes?'

'I just wanted to say how much I appreciated your help with Harry. I was at my wits' end.'

'It wasn't a problem.' And after his initial awkwardness it hadn't been.

He thought about her ridiculous dance, glanced at the coloured nappies flapping in the breeze and recalled the sense of well-being that had flooded him as he'd sung 'Fernando'. He remembered the weight of his nephew resting against his chest. Something dead in him had come alive.

And that something now noticed how a good night's sleep in combination with the sun and fresh air had painted new colour into Sapphie's cheeks. She had hair the colour of honey, and skin the colour of honeycomb. He found himself measuring the plump fullness of her bottom lip and wondering if she'd taste like honey too. Or peaches? That fragrance reached out to wrap around him now.

Emerald eyes widened at whatever they saw reflected in his face. Those generous lips parted the merest fraction.

If he…

Green fire suddenly snapped out at him. Those lips formed a hard, tight line.

He blinked.

She backed up a step, pointed behind her, her gaze sliding away. 'I, umm, should really go check on Harry. He went down for a nap right after breakfast and he'll probably wake any moment now.'

She turned and set off for the house. Fast. Beneath that oversized shirt of hers Liam could make out the outline of her backside. Something inside him stirred. He swung away with an oath. That was precisely why he didn't want a woman here at Newarra.

Trouble with a capital T.

Sapphie clocked the exact moment Liam pushed his plate away. He'd be gone again soon, and then she could breathe easier again.

'Thanks, Beattie, that hit the spot.'

Beattie glanced up from loading the dishwasher. 'Young Sapphie there's the one you should be thanking. She insisted on taking care of lunch. She helped me with the baking this morning too. She's a dab hand in the kitchen, she is.'

When Liam turned his gaze to Sapphie, she did her best not to fidget. 'Thank you, Sapphie.'

She shrugged and wiped the Vegemite smears from Harry's face and hands, tried to ignore the way Liam's voice had lifted all the hairs on her arms. 'It was nothing. Just a few sandwiches.' She leapt to her feet. 'I'd best fix Harry's bottle and put him down for a nap.'

Liam didn't rise. He didn't leave the table. Her skin prickled some more. She rubbed Harry's back while she waited for the milk to warm, but she wasn't sure who she was trying to reassure—Harry or herself.

She jumped when the microwave dinged. Clutching Harry and his bottle, she fled to the sanctuary of the nursery.

'Here we go, Harry.' She laid him in his cot. He clutched Horsie close and stared about the room with wide, wary eyes. When she started to sing his eyes fastened on her face. He took his bottle then, and with a sigh closed his eyes. His breathing grew rhythmic, his hold on the stuffed horse eased.

'Sleep tight,' she whispered, her heart aching, still bruised and raw from the news that Harry's daddy was dead. She brushed a lock of hair from his face.

Liam rose the moment she re-entered the kitchen. It made her heart beat a little harder, a little faster. She'd thought he'd have returned to work by now. Had hoped he would. She'd been too aware of him during lunch. Uncomfortably aware. Beneath her long sleeves her skin prickled.

'I was hoping we could have a talk.' He didn't smile. His big body didn't unbend.

A talk? With photographic precision, she recalled the look he'd sent her earlier in the yard—awareness and approval turning to hunger. Blood thundered in her ears.

She didn't want that.

She didn't want that with any man.

Do you really think he'd force his attentions on you?

No. She drew the admission from the depths of herself— reluctantly but honestly. That didn't stop her heart pounding harder and faster whenever he was near, though. It didn't stop her from not wanting to be alone with him. He upset her equilibrium in a way no man ever had, and at the moment she needed to keep her balance—for Harry's sake.

'Sapphie?'

She realised she'd been staring at him. She moistened her lips. 'What do you want to talk about?'

'Harry.'

Oh!

'Beattie has made us up a tray of coffee. She took it through to the living room.'

He motioned that she should precede him. There was nothing for it but to surrender. She led the way, settled on the sofa. Liam lowered his big frame into his armchair, steepled his hands beneath his chin. Neither one of them made a move to pour the coffee.

'You said you wanted to talk about Harry?' she prompted. The silence was drawing her nerves tight. The longer she looked at him the harder it was to drag her gaze away. There was a certain pleasure to be had in…in looking at him. But she didn't trust in it.

'Yes.' He paused. When he spoke again, his words reverberated in the quiet of the room, even though he spoke softly. 'Sapphie, I'd like you and Harry to stay on for a bit.'

The very quietness of his words carried an impact that had her momentarily speechless. She didn't know why he wanted them to stay, but she could see how much it meant to him.

'Please consider it,' he continued. 'We need to organise DNA tests, and there's Harry future to consider.' He leant forward, held her gaze. 'I would like an opportunity to get to know my nephew.'

It was a reasonable request. She bit her lip. Her financial situation wouldn't allow her an extended visit. 'How long are we talking, here, Liam?'

'I'd like you to stay for at least another week, but if you could see your way clear to stay for a fortnight…?'

A fortnight? That would be pushing her resources to the limits. But for Harry's sake…

'You see, a fortnight would see me out of a bind.' He grimaced. 'In fact, you'd be doing me a favour.'

'Favour?'

He rose and checked through the door before returning to his chair. 'I don't want Beattie overhearing.'

She frowned. 'Beattie? Why?'

'Has she told you her daughter is pregnant?'

She grinned as she remembered Beattie's excitement earlier that morning. 'She can't wait to be a grandma again. She said she's taking leave to be there for the birth.'

'Yeah, in a fortnight.' He paused. 'Did she tell you there've been complications with this pregnancy?'

'No!'

'Nothing too serious,' he assured her. 'But I know both Beattie and her daughter would feel a whole lot better if Beattie were there with her now.'

'Why doesn't she go?'

He scowled. 'Some nonsense about refusing to leave me alone in the house. Apparently I'll brood myself into an early grave, or some such garbage. My head stockman and his wife are moving into the homestead from the out station when Beattie takes her leave, but I can't ask them to move in here sooner, because we're mustering at that end of the property at the moment. If Beattie knew you and Harry would be here for the next fortnight, she'd go off to her daughter's with an easy mind.'

'You're offering me the post of housekeeper for a fortnight?'

'I am. You have experience of a large cattle station. The pay's good—includes food and lodgings—and the work isn't too onerous. You'd be doing a good thing for Beattie and her daughter and…'

'And?' she prompted.

'You'd be doing a good thing for me too.'

She leant forward. 'This means a lot to you, doesn't it?

'Yes.'

One word. But such a wealth of meaning behind it. It suddenly hit her—could she give Liam the chance she'd never had with her own child? She would never deny anyone that opportunity. She certainly couldn't deny it to Harry's uncle.

Or Harry.

Her heart started to pound. If Bryce had come forward when she'd been a child and claimed her as his daughter it would have made all the difference in the world to her. But he hadn't, and she'd grown up without a father. Even now she could feel that lack in her life. Liam wasn't Harry's father, but it didn't mean he couldn't become a father figure to Harry, did it?

New hope sprang to life inside her. 'Why is it so important to you, Liam?'

He was quiet for a long moment. 'You said your sister wanted Harry's father to take over his care.'

'That's right.'

'She wants to give up all access to him? All claim on him?' She swallowed. 'Yes.'

'Why?'

His frown didn't make his face look grimmer, just…bewildered. A weight settled on her shoulders. Her temples started to pound. 'She thinks it's what's best for Harry.'

He pinched the bridge of his nose. 'Right.' He pulled his hand away. 'Sapphie, are you planning to adopt Harry?'

She flinched away in horror at his suggestion. 'Me? No!'

An ache grew so big inside her she thought it might swallow her whole. Over the course of the last few days she'd grown to love Harry more than…more than she'd thought possible. She'd lay her life down in an instant to protect him if she had to—without hesitation. His happiness and his welfare—they were all that mattered.

She swallowed back a wall of panic. It would not be in Harry's best interests for her to adopt him. She'd had an abortion, and she didn't deserve—

And look at what a hash she'd made of raising Emmy. What further proof did she need? Oh, no, she was the worst person in the world to take over Harry's care.

Liam shot forward on his seat to stare at her, colour slashing high on his cheekbones. 'Why not?'

His words were bullets, tearing through the sorest places in her heart. For a moment it hurt too much even to breathe. When she was sure she wouldn't cry, she lifted her chin. 'I'm not adopting Harry, Liam. Just leave it at that.'

He stared at her for a long moment, and then his eyes blazed. 'Fine. Then I will. I'll adopt Harry.'

Sapphire gulped. Why did his words leave her stomach churning? Why did she suddenly want to race into the nursery, snatch Harry up and hold him close?

The fire that raged in Liam's eyes was too much, too intense. And she didn't understand it.

'Why would you want to adopt Harry?' she whispered. 'What makes you think you're capable of giving him what he needs?' Her fingers curled, her nails biting into her palms. He had to see exactly what adopting Harry would mean. She had to force him to see it. 'Liam, you can't even talk about what happened to Lucas.'

His head reared back. 'What does that prove?'

She stared at him for a moment, then swallowed. 'You even need to ask?'

He shot to his feet. She heard the curse he let fly even though he covered his mouth with the back of his hand.

He shoved his hands in his pockets and paced the length of the room, paused, and then paced back again. He fell into his chair, and was quiet for so long she didn't think he was going to say anything. Then, 'Twenty months ago Lucas was involved in a car accident. My mother had organised a party here at Newarra. She'd invited all the local debutantes. She was playing matchmaker.' He paused. 'I was divorced five years ago. She was hoping I'd find myself a new wife. I was far from impressed.'

The twist of his lips told her he hadn't been the least interested in finding a new wife.

'She ordered me to collect a carload of guests, all women, from a neighbouring property—a six-hour round trip. I talked Lucas into going instead, saying there was too much work to do around the station.'

He paused. 'The accident report said Lucas swerved—trying to miss a roo, probably—and that the car rolled. He broke his back.'

She closed her eyes. She knew where he was going with this. She'd played this game too.

She opened her eyes again. 'Do you blame your mother for Lucas's accident?'

His head shot up. 'No!'

'Then you can't blame yourself.'

'I was a better driver than him, and—'

'And what if…? All the what-ifs in the world won't bring him back. It doesn't make you responsible for his accident.'

He stared at her, but she didn't think he actually saw her. 'The accident left him crippled and in a wheelchair. He spent nearly ten months in hospital before coming home to Newarra. He was only home for six weeks when…'

She moistened her lips. 'When what?'

He pushed out of his chair. 'I should've seen what was happening to him.'

She watched him pace and her chest started to tighten. 'What are you talking about?'

'Depression.' He flung an arm out. 'I should've seen it coming. He was always so active, and all of a sudden he was stuck in a wheelchair. The family—we all tiptoed around him. But I should've given him something to do, made him feel useful again, but he was still recovering from the accident and I wanted to protect him. I thought there was plenty of time, but…'

A growing sense of horror started to unfurl in her stomach. 'But what?'

He didn't answer.

'Liam?'

'He killed himself.' He spun around. 'Lucas committed suicide!'

Her hand flew to her mouth.

'And I should've seen it coming.'

'No, you're wrong! That's not your fault either, Liam.'

'I should've taken better care of my little brother.' He dragged a hand back through his hair. 'I owe him, Sapphie.'

'*Owe* him?'

'I owe my whole family. My mother can't step foot on Newarra any more because this is where it happened. Even though Newarra had been her home for over forty years. I owe them all.'

What did he mean *owed* them?

'Let me adopt Lucas's son. Give me a chance to put it all to rights.'

'No!' She leapt off the sofa, shaking with the horror of all he'd been through…and the horror of what he was proposing now. 'Babies aren't sticking plaster, Liam. Harry's sole purpose in life is *not* to make you and your mother feel better! He's a baby—a little boy—and you can't thrust that kind of responsibility onto him. He should be loved for himself, not as a…as a replacement for Lucas.'

The tan leached from his face. 'I—'

'It is *not* Harry's responsibility to make you happy. It's your responsibility to make *him* happy.'

'I'm not—'

'What makes you think you're such great father material anyway? You can barely crack a smile, let alone laugh.

What kind of environment is *that* for a little boy to grow up in, huh?'

'What other options does Harry have?'

His words stopped her dead. Her legs gave out, dropping her back to the sofa. Harry's options? With his mother in jail, his father dead, and an aunt who was worse than useless? A foster family? The very thought broke her heart.

'Do you doubt that I would love him?'

She didn't know. There were shadows in this man—shadows she wasn't sure he could overcome.

There were shadows in her too. *Yeah, but she wasn't proposing to adopt Harry.*

And then she remembered the way he'd sung in the early hours of this morning. If the man could sing, could he learn to laugh again? Could he learn to be a proper father to Harry?

He loomed in front of her now, his bulk cutting out the light from the French doors. 'Sapphie, we need to talk about this.'

Slowly she nodded, tried to find the strength to straighten her spine. 'Yes, we do.' When he didn't move she added, 'But I don't want to talk with you towering over me.'

He immediately sat—on the floor—giving her the height advantage. It was a nice thing to do.

'I should go home and talk to Emmy—find out what she wants me to do.'

'If you go home now, all you'll be able to tell her is about Lucas's death. If you stay…'

'If I stay?'

'You can tell her about me and Newarra. If I can prove to you that I can bond with Harry and give him a good life here then it might give her an option she hasn't considered.'

His words made sense.

'I don't know how serious Emmy is about having Harry adopted. New mums sometimes need a little time out. She could have postnatal depression. She could be rethinking her decision right this very moment.'

Sapphie recalled the resolution in Emmy's eyes and pulled her hands through her hair. 'She's serious.'

'But, apart from all that, doesn't Harry deserve to know his father's family too?'

Sapphie recalled all those photographs in the family album Liam had shown her only yesterday. Harry deserved the very best life could offer. Could Liam give it to him?

He reached over and took her hand. 'Don't I at least deserve a chance?'

The moment he took her hand Liam knew he shouldn't have. It trembled in his, and the combination of her softness and warmth created an ache so deep and sweet it took all his strength not to lean across and kiss her.

Kiss her? His pulse kicked in instant response and all his senses fired to life.

He tried to draw breath into his body without betraying how starved for air it was. He couldn't prevent his gaze from dropping to her lips; he couldn't stop himself from wondering what it would be like to taste them.

Her eyes turned a deep luminous green and her tongue snaked out to moisten those lips—generous, full lips that promised—

She shot back from him, snatching her hand from his. She scooted along to the far end of the sofa, held up the coffee pot. 'Did you want coffee? It'll go cold soon.'

'No, thank you.' He didn't think he could stomach coffee at the moment.

She dropped the pot back to the tray. He couldn't get the scent of her out of his nostrils.

'Then do you mind if we move outside?' She was already on her feet and halfway to the door. 'We may as well take advantage of the fresh air.'

He stared after her, recognised the tension in her spine, the tightness. His teeth ground together. He was not in the habit of forcing his attentions on unwilling women. Surely she realised that?

Would she be unwilling, though? The thought filtered though him—insidious, tempting. Perhaps that tenseness was because she was holding herself on as tight a rein as him?

He shot to his feet with a curse. It didn't matter whether she wanted him or not. He wasn't going there. This woman had *for ever* written all over her. He'd tried for ever and it didn't work. He wasn't going through that again. He should be concerning himself with guaranteeing his nephew's future. Nothing else.

With a grim nod, he followed her out to the veranda.

She stood at the railing, hands folded in front of her as she stared out at the garden. This had been his mother's favourite spot. Even at the height of summer it felt cool out here. An illusion, perhaps, created by the two giant pepper trees that dominated the lawn on this side of the house. Their shadows, lengthening now as the afternoon waned, created huge swathes of dappled shade, their long strands swaying on the smallest breeze.

'Sapphie?' He motioned to an old-fashioned wrought-iron and wooden bench, overlaid with a thick pad. Sapphie ignored it to lean over the veranda balustrade. Liam remembered how she hadn't wanted to talk to him while he'd towered over her, so he lowered his frame to the bench instead, and waited.

Finally she turned and leant back against the railing, her hands going behind her to grip it. 'You're right, Liam. Harry *does* deserve to know all his family.'

Hope lifted through him. If only Sapphie would give him a chance. He wanted to give Harry the childhood Lucas would have wanted for his son. Liam owed Lucas that.

'Lucas would have wanted Harry to grow up out here.' He wanted her to know that.

He didn't know why he couldn't say it out loud—perhaps

it meant too much—but he burned to give Harry the child-hood he and Belinda had planned for their own children.

'You're wrong, Liam. What Lucas would want is for whoever adopts Harry to love him like a son.'

Like a son. Her words stabbed him.

'Can you do that?'

Yes! A thousand times yes! But he couldn't push the words out of his throat. He remembered his feelings of inadequacy last night when he'd first held Harry and his conviction wavered. Sapphie had dealt with a screaming, crying child for six hours. If the need arose, could he? On his own?

'Sid told me you were a good man. Beattie said you were a good man. So did Jared and Anna. But it doesn't necessarily follow that you're the right man for this job.'

'I can try!' The words burst from him. 'If you'll stay, it'll give Harry and I a chance to get to know one another.'

He rose and planted his hands on his hips. 'If you stay on at Newarra as housekeeper for the next two weeks you'll get an insider's view of life here, and then you'll be able to make an informed decision as to whether Harry can be happy here...have a good life here. That's all I'm asking, Sapphie—for a chance.'

He wanted to reach out and take her hand in his again. He dragged in a breath and resisted the urge. 'Will you stay?'

For a brief moment she wavered, and then she smiled and it stole all his held breath. 'Yes, Liam,' she finally said. 'Harry and I—we'll stay for the next fortnight.'

CHAPTER FIVE

SAPPHIE skipped down the back steps, jumping off the last one and making for the clothesline, her step light and springy. She couldn't account for the energy that fizzed through her, leaving her revitalised, invigorated, but a bubble of optimism was growing inside her—dislodging and lifting the weight from her shoulders.

She hadn't caught up on all her sleep yet.

Harry's future was far from assured.

But things looked brighter than they had at midnight last night.

Harry had smiled at her more than once. He'd even hugged her! Liam had sung 'Fernando'. The afternoon was all golden, violet and orange. The air was still, and scented with clean earth and warm rock. The sun was benign. The gentle chattering of a flock of northern rosellas came from the pepper trees. She flung her arms out, tossed her head back, and dragged it all into her lungs.

She loved this part of the world!

Of course you do. You're Bryce Curran's daughter.

The thought made her stumble. Out of the corner of her eye she caught movement and recoiled, but she wasn't quick enough. The ground beneath her left foot reared up and hissed at her.

She snatched her foot back, so startled that she shot backwards with two awkward half-hops before her heels, failing to find purchase, shot out from beneath her and sent her crashing spectacularly to the ground.

She lay there, gasping, the air forced out of her lungs by the impact. The offending piece of ground tore away from her on its hind legs, tail swishing behind it. A frilled-neck lizard! She should laugh—the imagined threat was no real threat at all.

She *would* laugh. Just as soon as she got her breath back. Just as soon as her heart rate returned to normal.

She tried to force her body to relax, tried not to fight the effects of being winded. She knew her breath would return faster if she surrendered for a moment and unclenched her body.

Impossible.

Then came the sound of heavy footsteps running towards her, and her heart-rate almost exploded as a shadow loomed over her, blocking the sun. 'That was one heck of a fall! Are you all right?'

A big, broad, *male* body leaned over her. Strong, powerful. Overpowering. Fear welled in her chest. Panic clawed at her throat. She tried to back away from it, but pain gripped her lower leg, momentarily disabling her.

Idiot! She'd let her guard down. This was a working station. There'd be stockman, ringers…men she didn't know. She tried to ignore the pain, did what she could to push away from the threat of this body, tried to dislodge the lump from her throat to open her mouth and scream as loud as she could.

'What are you doing?'

Exasperation laced the voice as the shape crouched down beside her. He threw off his hat and—

Liam! It was Liam!

She closed her eyes and let relief flood her.

Oh, no. She snapped her eyes open. She would not make the same mistake twice. After all, what did she *really* know about Liam Stapleton?

'He's a good man,' Sid had said.

'He's a good man,' Beattie had said

'He's a good man,' Anna and Jared had said.

Yeah, well… She'd thought Jonathon had been a good man too. It hadn't stopped him from raping her.

Liam is not going to rape you.

'Sapphie?'

She swallowed, and did what she could to rein in her panic. 'I…I stepped on a frilled-neck lizard.'

'I saw. We've a pair of them.' His lips twisted. 'They've the whole of the Kimberley, over 420,000 square kilometres of land to choose from, and yet they decide to take up residence in my pepper trees.' He paused. Those Kimberley-sky eyes of his narrowed. 'You look like you've seen a ghost.'

'It scared the living daylights out of me!'

One eyebrow rose.

'It's being winded,' she muttered. 'I hate it. Not being able to breathe like that.'

But she had her breath back now. She went to push to her feet, but fell back with a gasp as pain clamped around her right calf and refused to let go.

'What is it?' Liam leant towards her, his voice sharp.

'Cramp,' she gritted out from between her teeth. 'I just need to walk it out.'

'You're not walking on that leg until I've taken a look at it. Put your arm around my shoulders.'

She forgot all about the pain. 'What?'

'Either you put your arm around my shoulders so I can help you hobble over to the steps, where I can take a decent look at you, or I'll carry you. Your call.'

She gaped at him.

'Sapphie, we're miles from medical help. If you've hurt your leg I don't want to make it worse. We don't take those kinds of chances out here. If you've twisted your knee or ankle badly, Beattie is going to have to stay. You'll need help with Harry.'

'No! Beattie has to go to Kununurra to be with her daughter. She was so excited.'

'Why don't we just check the leg first? All right?'

There didn't seem to be anything else to do but submit.

'Give me your hands.'

She pulled in a breath, let it out again, and did as he said.

'Don't put any weight on that leg,' he warned as he pulled her to her feet and slid an arm around her waist to steady her.

Cautiously, she reached up to hold onto his shoulder. Her breath caught and her fingers dug into firm flesh as the cramp caught hold with renewed vigour.

But, despite the pain, with every hobbled step towards the back steps she grew more and more aware of the man beside her—his hardness, his strength…the latent power and heat that he generated. With every step her hip, her side, her thigh, bumped against his hip, his side, his thigh…

Her heart pounded and her throat went dry. The hand at her waist held her against him…firm yet gentle.

'Easy,' he murmured, lowering her to the steps.

She tried to say thank you, but her throat wouldn't work.

'I'm going to take your shoe off.'

She stared at the lean, tanned hands as they worked her sneaker free, and had to fight the urge to not pull away.

He peeled off her sock. 'It's not swollen.' His fingers probed the bare flesh of her ankle. 'Does this hurt?'

The cramp took hold again. She held herself so tense she was amazed her whole body didn't cramp up. 'It's not my ankle. It's my calf,' she ground out.

Her heart fluttered all the way into her throat when he started to roll up her jeans. 'What are you doing?' she squeaked.

'I need to take a look.'

He kept rolling her jeans, almost to the knee. She reached down to push his hands away, to rub the calf muscle herself, but he batted her hands away. Before she could protest further he stretched out her leg, flexed her ankle, and then his long, lean fingers started to massage her calf, working the muscle, running up and then down the bare flesh of her leg.

Sapphie fell back on her elbows, fighting the conflicting desire to leap out of this man's grasp or to lean back further and groan her relief as the pain eased.

With a superhuman effort, she did neither.

Liam glanced up. 'Better?'

She nodded.

His fingers didn't stop. They continued to rub and massage her calf, and Sapphie found her limbs growing languid and warm. She found herself wishing she'd had time for a leg wax before she'd left Perth.

She stiffened. That was the craziest thought she'd ever had in her life! She didn't care what Liam thought of her legs. She didn't want him to find them attractive or…or otherwise.

'I…uh…' She tried to detach her leg from his grasp. 'It's fine now.'

'Not yet.' He rotated her foot clockwise, then anti-clockwise. 'Does that hurt?'

'No.' The word emerged short and just a tiny bit breathy.

He bent her knee. 'Or that?'

'No.' She couldn't stand it any more. She pushed his hands away and moved up a step. 'I told you, it was just a cramp.'

He pursed his lips. He didn't straighten from his crouch.

'What?' she said, defensive hackles rising as he continued to stare at her.

'That cramp—it could've been caused by the sudden change in direction.'

'Uh-huh.' She started to unroll the leg of her jeans.

'Cramps can also be caused by dehydration.'

'I'm not dehydrated. I've drunk plenty of water since I arrived. Not to mention tea.'

He stared at the collar of her shirt, at the long sleeves. 'I bet you've perspired plenty out again in *that* get-up.'

She sucked in a breath, shot to her feet. 'What I'm wearing is no concern of yours!'

'Can you walk on that leg?'

'Of course I can.' She welcomed the change in topic. She took a few steps along the veranda to prove it. 'See?' The muscle was tight, but not enough to stop her from getting about.

'Good, then come with me.'

He strode through the back door. She followed more slowly. Beattie smiled at them as they passed through the kitchen.

Liam led her down an unfamiliar corridor and flung open a door. 'This is Lacey's room.'

His sister?

'I know it's coming on to winter in Perth. I know you didn't plan on spending a whole fortnight in the Kimberley and packed accordingly.' He moved into the room to throw open a wardrobe door. 'Lacey won't mind if you borrow a few things while you're here.'

The wardrobe revealed a row of dresses and skirts.

He pulled open a dresser drawer. It was full of shorts. Another drawer revealed shirts—frilly shirts, T-shirts, shirts with scooped necks…with plunging necklines. In all the colours of the rainbow.

She stared at them. Then she backed up a step, her fingers flying to her top button. 'No, thank you. I'll make do with my own things.'

And then she turned and fled.

At the end of the working day Liam reached for the handle of the back door, but stopped short of opening it, suddenly aware of how his hand trembled and how his knees were none too steady.

He dragged in a breath. He was a grown man. A baby shouldn't intimidate him.

How Lachlan and Lacey would laugh if they could see their supposedly fearless big brother now. His lips twisted. How Lucas would laugh.

He dragged off his hat, scraped a forearm across his brow,

then hung the hat on its peg. He curled his fingers around the door handle, pulled it open and forced himself through it. And stopped short again.

Sapphie sat on the floor, her back against one of the kitchen cupboards, with her legs stretched out in front of her. Harry stood between her legs, his hands in hers for support. When he heard Liam, he fell onto his nappy-clad bottom and crawled into Sapphie's lap. Her arms went about him in the most natural gesture in the world.

Can you love Harry like your own son? His gut clenched. He'd given up on the idea of children—had pushed the pictures that word evoked to the outer reaches of his consciousness, where he'd buried them.

He stared at the baby. Could Harry be his second chance? A part of him wanted to erect barriers around his heart, protect it against the possibility of disappointment…pain. But if he wanted to win Harry's trust he couldn't do that.

Can you love him like your own son?

He didn't know. He wanted to say yes, but…

He didn't know what to do. Sapphie was staring at him, a frown in her eyes. He didn't know what to say. She pursed her lips and glanced down at Harry, and then she smiled. Just like that—easy and without hardship. Without caution.

'Look, Harry, it's Uncle Liam!' She picked up one of Harry's arms and waved it at Liam. 'Hello, Uncle Liam.'

Liam waved back, tried to smile. 'Hello, Harry. Hello, Sapphie.' He lowered the bags he carried to the floor.

Her eyes narrowed, but she kept her voice cheerful and sing-song. 'Are you still quite sure you want to make friends with Harry here?'

'Yes.' *She* might manage the sing-song thing, but he couldn't—not when it felt as if the weight of the world was pressing down on his shoulders. He had to prove to her that he could be a good father figure to Harry. He had to. For

Lucas's sake. For his entire family's sake. He couldn't let them down. 'Yes,' he repeated.

He had a feeling the raw need showed on his face, because her eyes softened. With one lithe movement she rose, Harry balanced on her hip, and sashayed over to him. 'Right, let's get on with it then.'

He stiffened. What the heck...?

She smelt of baby powder and chopped onions and some herb—rosemary. She smelt like home and rest.

'Auntie Sapphie kisses Horsie.' She seized the stuffed horse and gave it a loud kiss. 'And now Uncle Liam kisses Horsie.'

She held out the stuffed toy to him, and for a moment her eyes danced with a delicious mixture of mischief and fun. Liam grinned. He couldn't help it. He took the toy and planted a kiss to Horsie's nose.

'And Harry kisses Horsie.'

Harry had watched these proceedings with solemn caution. He glanced at Liam, and then at the toy. Very tentatively he took Horsie from Liam and cuddled it close, making loud smacking sounds with his lips.

'Now Sapphie kisses Harry.' She kissed Harry's cheek. 'And so does Uncle Liam.'

Liam started. She nodded her encouragement. He leant in and kissed the top of Harry's head, then moved back again. Fast. He told himself he didn't want his bulk to frighten the child.

Sapphie jiggled Harry on her hip. 'And now Harry kisses Uncle Liam.'

For a moment Liam thought Harry really did mean to lean across and plant a wet kiss on his cheek. He held his breath and waited, but at the last moment Harry hid his face in Sapphie's neck.

Sapphie grinned and winked. 'That went better than I thought.' She pulled out a chair and sat. 'I'm just planting the idea in his head at the moment, letting him know who his friends are.'

He fell into the chair opposite, his heart pounding. 'So I shouldn't be mortally wounded by rejection, then?'

'Not unless you want to be a drama queen about it.'

That had him grinning again. She wasn't the kind of woman who'd let a body get away with anything.

Maybe if she'd kissed *him* first, to set an example for Harry… His thought processes slammed to a halt as his mind lost itself in images of her kissing him…and him kissing her.

'These things take time.'

He'd take her word on that.

'Beattie get away okay?'

'Yep.' He'd just flown Beattie to Kununurra in the station's single-engine Cessna. 'She's very grateful to you.'

'Pshaw!' She dismissed that with one flick of her wrist, and for some reason he found himself grinning again. Or was that grinning *still*?

He tried to ramp up the tension inside himself again, to maintain his guard, but it had been a long day, and the kitchen smelt so good that almost against his will his shoulders loosened. He glanced around. 'Something smells great.'

'Ah, that reminds me. I have a housekeeping question for you.'

Her eyes danced. Harry sat on her lap, quietly chewing one of Horsie's ears, but at her tone he glanced up at her and his little face lit up with a smile. Liam found he couldn't look away from either one of them. 'What?'

'Do cattlemen get sick of steak for dinner? I mean, you work with cattle all day—mustering them, drafting and branding them, not to mention breeding them. And, as I found a cold room today, I'm guessing you probably butcher your own meat. Don't you get sick of all that…beef?'

'Nope.'

'Don't you dream of a nice piece of fish or some crispy fried chicken? Or hanker for a Chinese takeaway or a pizza?'

He leant back and stretched his legs out. 'Nope.' Not

strictly speaking true, but he found he enjoyed teasing her. His grin grew. Besides, in his book a juicy steak would always come out on top.

She shook her head in mock regret. 'I'm afraid you're going to be sadly disappointed this evening, when you find out steak isn't on the menu.'

He doubted that.

'We're having lamb stew. I didn't know what time you'd get back, and I figured a lamb stew could just bubble away until we were ready to eat. I don't care what you say—hot lamb stew beats cold steak any day. Oh, and I made cornbread.'

He blinked. 'Cornbread?'

'We need something to dunk in our stew. It always went down a treat when my mother made it at Jarndirri. When I saw the packet of polenta in the pantry I couldn't resist.'

'It sounds great.' It did. And it made him realise how long it had been since he'd sat in this kitchen and felt relaxed…happy.

He glanced at Harry. Moved his gaze to Sapphie. His spine stiffened. This might look the picture of perfect domestic bliss but—

'Stop analysing everything and just enjoy a well-earned rest at the end of a hard day's work,' Sapphie chided, as if she could see right inside his head.

The idea had him rolling his shoulders.

She rose to slide Harry into his highchair. Panic flashed across Harry's face, and it reached right inside Liam's chest to squeeze his heart in a grip that had him breathing hard.

Sapphie didn't blink an eye. She clapped her hands and beamed. 'We have to teach Uncle Liam what to give you for dinner, Harry.'

Harry didn't smile, but he clapped his hands to copy Sapphie and the panic drained from his face. Liam slumped. In a few short days Harry and Sapphie had bonded. How would *he* ever know what to do the way she seemed to? Could *he* make Harry happy? Make him feel secure and safe?

His thoughts whirled to a halt when Sapphie launched into another ABBA song, the most off-key rendition he'd ever heard. It built that grin back up inside him. She danced across the room to the cutlery drawer and returned with three spoons. She handed one to him, one to Harry, and dropped the third to the table.

She danced over to another cupboard and pulled out two jars of baby food. He didn't know how she could radiate so much colour when she wore nothing but a pair of denim jeans and a big buttoned-down white shirt.

She broke off her song to hold the jars out towards the table. 'Chicken or beef, Harry?'

'Beef,' Liam said promptly. Harry banged his spoon on the tray of the highchair. 'See—he agrees with me.'

She heated the jar in the microwave and then danced back over to the table and set about feeding Harry. Liam turned the spoon he held over and over in his fingers.

In between silly baby talk with Harry, Sapphie told Liam everything she and Harry had got up to that day, while he'd been flying back and forth from Kununurra. They'd explored the house, the veranda and the garden; they'd had a picnic under the pepper trees. He found himself half wishing he could have stayed here and… And what? He pushed the thought away.

When Sapphie spooned out the last of the baby food, Liam suddenly remembered. 'I brought presents back.'

'Ooh, Harry—presents!' Sapphie rubbed her hands together. 'I love presents!' She grinned at Liam. 'So you remembered the caramel topping, then?'

He had—it had been her special request. She'd said that if she was staying for a whole fortnight she couldn't do without caramel topping. He lifted it out and set it on the table. 'But that's not the present. Who first—you or Harry?'

Her eyes went round. 'You bought me a present?'

That settled it. He reached into the bag at his feet, rifled through the newspapers and farm journals he'd bought as well, then pulled out a DVD and handed it to her.

Her face lit up. '*Mamma Mia*! I love this movie. Ooh, Harry, guess what we're watching tomorrow afternoon.' She did a little dance in her seat and Harry smiled and banged his spoon some more. 'I found the theatre room. It's wonderful.'

The theatre room. He hadn't been in there since... 'We had it put in after Lucas's accident.' He'd hoped the big screen and surround sound would...

'Liam?'

He shook himself. 'Now for Harry's present.' He pulled a stuffed toy cow from the bag. Harry's eyes went as wide as Sapphie's had. He stared at the toy, and then at Liam, in wonder. Then he held out his arms, and very gently Liam placed the stuffed animal into them.

'Ta!' Harry said, without being prompted.

Liam's chest puffed out. 'You're welcome,' he said. 'Only we are not calling it Cowie.' He reached over and pressed the cow's ear, and a deep 'moo' filled the room.

Sapphie burst out laughing. Harry swung to her and held out his new toy, a grin stretching across his face. 'Moo-Moo,' he said.

'Moo-Moo is the perfect name,' she agreed. 'Now you have a friend for Horsie.' She turned to Liam. 'Thank you, that was really thoughtful.'

Liam surveyed Harry, pursed his lips. 'When is he going to smile at me?'

'The day after tomorrow.'

The precision of her reply made him blink. He snorted. 'You can't know that.'

She leapt up to rummage through the cupboard again. 'Why not?'

'You could be wrong.'

'Ah, but *you* can't know that.'

He closed his mouth. She was right.

'Ta-da!' She waved a tin at Harry. 'Chocolate custard!'

Harry waved his arms and kicked his legs, his whole face lighting up. A swell of protectiveness surged through Liam, leaving him breathless, boneless.

Sapphie winked at him. 'The way to a man's heart…'

'His stomach?'

'Absolutely! Chocolate custard is to die for.'

She peeled back the lid, scooped out a spoonful and popped it in her mouth. She closed her eyes in what looked like ecstasy, and Liam went breathless and boneless all over again.

'Come on—your turn.'

He came to to find Sapphie holding out a spoonful of custard for him.

'All Harry's friends eat chocolate custard.'

He figured that was a hint…or a warning. He opened his mouth and let her feed him the custard. And all he could think was how her lips had closed around this same spoon, how slowly she'd pulled this spoon from her mouth…how ripe and full her lips were.

Their eyes locked. Hers went round and huge. They dropped to his lips and his stomach tightened.

She pulled back with a squeak.

'Yum,' Harry announced to Liam.

Liam didn't know if it was a question, a statement, or a demand to be fed. 'Yum,' he agreed. He watched as Sapphie fed Harry two laden spoonfuls.

'Yum,' Harry said again.

Liam nodded. 'Yum.' He couldn't remember what the custard had tasted like, only the look in Sapphie's eyes. And Harry was right—*yum*.

'Ooh, Uncle Liam knows this game.' Sapphie pushed the tin into Liam's hands. 'You finish feeding Harry while I get his bottle ready.'

Did she really trust him to feed Harry? The little spoon, the little tin—they felt tiny in his big hands. He glanced at his nephew. Would he even let Liam feed him? It shocked him to realise how much it meant. Harry stared at him, then opened his mouth, obviously impatient for the next mouthful of custard.

Liam managed to manoeuvre a spoonful of the stuff to Harry's mouth without mishap. Harry smacked his lips together, swallowed, and opened his mouth for more. Liam's back straightened and his chest puffed out. He hadn't experienced such a sense of accomplishment in…

He couldn't remember when, and he didn't bother trying. For once he meant to do what Sapphie ordered and just enjoy the moment.

Sapphie leant against the kitchen bench and watched Liam feed Harry…and tried to stop her insides from turning to mush. There was something about a big broad-shouldered man with a little baby that tugged at a woman's insides.

There was something about Liam that tugged at her all over.

No! What on earth was she thinking? Sleep deprivation— that had to be it. She must still be sleep-deprived because…

Her throat tightened. Her heart started to pound. She tried to drag her eyes from the vee of Liam's workshirt, with its intriguing glimpse of curling dark hair, tried to shake off the languor that stole over her limbs. She didn't get *things* for flesh-and-blood men. She kept real men well and truly at arm's length. She only got *things*…crushes…for unattainable men—film stars, rock stars.

She would not develop a *thing* for Liam Stapleton!

It hit her then. Being alone with Liam in this big old homestead for the next fortnight. It didn't frighten her. Not the way it ought to. When he'd helped her to the steps yesterday, when he'd rubbed the cramp from her leg, anxiety for her personal safety had not been the emotion uppermost in her mind.

Because he's not the kind of man who would force a woman.

He was the kind of man who sang to help settle a baby to sleep.

She recalled how gently his fingers had probed her ankle…and she recalled the way he'd just looked at her over that tin of chocolate custard. The heat from his eyes had almost raised steam from her skin. He'd looked at her the way a man looked at a woman he desired. He did chaotic things to her blood.

She didn't want that!

She would not let that kind of chaos loose in her life.

What she had to do was help Harry and Liam bond—end of story. Anything else was…impossible.

'He likes to play choo-choo trains too,' she said, deliberately swinging away to warm the milk for Harry's bottle.

She had to turn back when Liam started making train noises, though. All his grimness had fallen away. Hope had sprung to his eyes, softening the lines that bracketed his mouth and fanned out from his eyes, making him look younger, giving her a picture of how he must have been before Lucas's death.

She found herself having to swallow a lump. 'Don't forget to feed Harry's friends. Horsie and Moo-Moo love chocolate custard as well.'

He knew that game too. He pretended to feed Harry's stuffed toys, and her insides turned to mush all over again. Get the baby's bottle ready, she ordered herself. Stop ogling.

She turned with the bottle just as Liam scraped the tin of custard clean. He held it up. 'I think he could go another tin of that stuff.'

She bit back a grin. 'I think you mean *you* could.'

He shrugged, and looked so delightfully nonplussed it took all the strength she had in her to not lean over and plant a kiss on the top of his head.

A crazy thought.

She wiped Harry's face clean and then lifted him out of

his highchair. The longing on Liam's face made her pause. 'Are you starving yet? Do you want dinner now, or can you hold off for a bit?'

'I can hold off.'

'Then go get your guitar and meet me in Harry's room.'

His smile vanished just like that. His shoulders tensed. It was as if she'd flicked a switch that had turned all the lights out and plunged him into darkness.

He shot to his feet. 'I'm going to take a shower.' He nodded towards Harry without looking at him. 'Take your time. I'm in no hurry for dinner.'

With that, he strode from the room. She stared after him, and all her previous warmth drained out of her.

He hasn't been in the nursery since...

Since when? She now wished she'd asked Beattie. Since his wife had left? Five years ago?

A chill crept through her. 'Oh, Harry, this isn't good.' If Liam refused to face his demons then...then this next fortnight was an exercise in futility. Liam was Harry's best hope. If he failed, Harry would be placed in the care of strangers.

She cuddled Harry close. 'Don't you worry, Harry. I'm not going to let that happen.'

CHAPTER SIX

SAPPHIE spooned a forkful of lamb stew into her mouth, chewed and swallowed, but she didn't really taste it. She glanced at Liam. He seemed to be enjoying it with all the gusto she lacked.

Watching him eat—watching the way his mouth closed around his fork, watching the way his nostrils flared as he relished the steam that rose into his face—tightened her stomach.

She put her fork down.

She picked her fork up.

Harry's uncle. That was what Liam was. That was how she had to think of him. And she needed Liam to bond with Harry—fast. The thought of Harry having to go through this process again with total strangers made her stomach rebel. But Liam wouldn't bond with Harry, not properly, if he refused to enter the nursery.

What if they changed the location of the nursery?

That wouldn't get to the root of the problem, though, would it? Liam had to confront his demons, not ignore them.

She speared a piece of carrot, swirled it through the gravy of the stew. *She* had to get him to confront those demons.

Nerves scythed through her. She dropped her fork to seize her glass of water.

Liam glanced up, gestured to his plate. 'This is really good.'

He looked surprised, as if he hadn't thought cooking would make it onto the list of her vast array of talents. For a moment she almost smiled. Then she thought he probably didn't even think she *had* a vast array of talents and her smile died before it had fully formed.

'It's Dana's recipe. My mum. She taught me to cook.'

'You call your mother Dana?'

'Called,' she corrected. 'Past tense. She died when I was eighteen.'

His eyes darkened. 'Sapphie, I'm sorry.'

She shrugged.

'Dana is what she preferred.' She picked up her fork again. 'Dana was a free spirit, a bit of a gypsy—we never stayed in one place for very long—and she was also a hippy. Hence our names.'

'Sapphire and Emerald,' he murmured. From his lips, their names sounded precious and wonderful.

'She called us her jewels.' Sapphie smiled at the memory. 'Emmy is very like her—inherited her wanderlust.' While all Sapphie had wanted was to settle down and grow some roots.

Liam sat back. 'Travelling around like that, it's no life for a child.'

'Oh, I don't know. As long as a child knows it's loved, I think all the rest is just window-dressing.'

'Do you really believe that?'

She thought back to her childhood, remembered how she'd yearned for the stability of a bricks and mortar house—of knowing what town she'd wake up in the next morning, what school she'd be expected to attend. But to agree with Liam seemed disloyal to her mother somehow, so she shrugged and said, 'Sure.'

Liam didn't say anything for a long moment. 'Sapphie, can I ask you a question?'

The intent in his eyes made her throat dry. She seized her glass of water again, drank long and hard, then nodded. 'Sure.'

'I see you with Harry, and I see how much you've come to love him in a very short space of time.'

She wanted to tell him *he* could love Harry just as well, just as easily and quickly, if only he'd take the chance. 'What's not to love? He's a baby, he's beautiful, and he's just so…lovable!'

'When I see you with Harry, I see how much you would love to raise him as your own.'

His words cut at her with scalpel-like precision. Her hand shook. 'I've already told you that's impossible.'

'Is it?'

'Yes.'

Emmy would never agree to it.

Emmy would be right!

It hit her then. Some time in the not too distant future she would have to give Harry up.

Fear gripped her. 'Liam, if we all—you, me and Emmy—decide that you're the best person to raise Harry, you *will* let me see him sometimes, won't you?'

He reached out and grabbed her hand, knocking over his glass of water as he did so. Neither one of them moved to right it or to mop up the mess.

'If I adopt him you can see Harry whenever you want. You can visit Newarra any time you like. Harry can have holidays with you in Perth. Sapphie, you and Harry *love* each other. You're important to each other. You are going to continue to be important to each other for the rest of your lives. I would never do anything to destroy that.'

Her eyes started to burn. 'Thank you.' She didn't deserve even that much, but she'd take it.

He let go of her hand, eased back. 'So…you wouldn't adopt Harry even if Emmy asked you to?'

If she told him the truth perhaps he'd stop tormenting her with impossible dreams. She reached out, righted the glass he'd knocked over. If she told him the truth perhaps he'd stop worrying that she, or fate, would snatch Harry away from him. Maybe then he'd find the strength to believe in Harry…love him.

'Emmy won't want me to adopt Harry, Liam. She'd never agree to it.' She knew that with her entire being.

A frown appeared in his eyes. 'Why not? You're great with him. She has to see that.'

For a moment it hurt too much even to look at him. She stared down at her plate of stew, and when she was sure she wouldn't cry she lifted her chin. 'I was eighteen when Dana died, but Emmy was only twelve. I was granted guardianship of her. I mean, there was no one else, but I didn't care. I didn't want to be separated from her.'

'It must've been hard.'

She shrugged. 'The neighbours were good to us, and a friend of Dana's helped out a lot.'

He paused. He set his fork by his plate. 'If you raised Emmy, why on earth wouldn't she want you to raise Harry too?'

Couldn't he see?

'Because I did such a bad job of it!'

She hadn't meant to snap. His jaw dropped. Her cheeks burned and her stomach rolled. She glanced down at her plate and tried to soften her tone.

'After Dana died we settled in Perth.' It was where Dana had spent the last weeks of her life, before the cancer had claimed her. 'I thought it would be best if Emmy had a regular school and…'

She pushed the hair off her face with both hands. 'I had to work two jobs just to meet the rent. There was never much money for treats, and I worked long hours. I didn't realise then, but not only had Emmy lost her mother she'd lost the way of life she'd loved too.'

It was just that Sapphie hadn't been able to live, not knowing where their next meal was coming from. She'd just wanted to give Emmy a home.

He leant towards her. 'You were young. You took care of her, loved her. You did your best.'

'I did what was best for *me*, not what was best for Emmy.' That's why Emmy would never give her custody of Harry. Why she'd be right not to.

Liam's eyes suddenly narrowed, as if he sensed there was more. 'What happened, Sapphie?'

Was she such an open book? She closed her eyes briefly. Full disclosure.

She opened her eyes and stared at her hands. 'A few days after her sixteenth birthday, Emmy ran away.'

'And?' he prompted.

'And nothing.' She glanced up. 'I searched everywhere for her. I lodged a missing person's report with the police. And until the money ran out I hired a private detective to try and find her. I never did.'

He went very still. 'When did you next see her?'

Her mouth went dry. 'Tuesday, when she handed me Harry and asked me to find his father. It seems I've failed at that too.'

Liam pushed his plate away. She could see how bad he felt for her. 'It's all in the past, Liam. I can't change it now. All I can do is try and work out what's best for Harry.'

He gave a heavy nod.

She pulled in a breath. 'Can I ask *you* a question now?'

He went as still as she had when he'd asked that self-same question. 'Yes?'

'I…umm…' She moistened her lips. 'Well, obviously I know you were married, because you told me you were divorced.'

His eyes suddenly blazed. 'Yes. So?'

'Did you and your wife have children together? Does Harry have—?'

'No.' His face closed up. He didn't add anything else.

'Yet you wanted children?'

'Yes.'

It was almost a snarl. Sapphie backed off. She picked up her fork and pointed to their food, biting back her questions. 'Eat up while it's still warm. I doubt cold stew is any more appetising than cold steak.'

They ate in silence. Not a comfortable silence either. It occurred to her that she rarely felt comfortable in his presence. Not threatened, just not comfortable. He was too big, too male. He drew too much of her attention. And since she'd acknowledged to herself that it was desire and curiosity that he aroused in her, not fear, she didn't quite know what to do. She had defences in place for fear, but not for this... longing.

'Okay, out with it!' He slammed his knife and fork to his plate. 'Just say whatever is on your mind and get it over with.'

Tell him she couldn't look at him without wanting to reach out and test the texture of his skin? The firmness of his flesh? Tell him she couldn't help wondering what it would be like to kiss him? Tell him her body had suddenly come alive out here in the isolation of the Kimberley when it had been happy hibernating for the last seven years?

Not in this lifetime!

Her usual breeziness, her defence against the world, deserted her. 'Nothing is on my mind!'

'You want to know why my marriage failed?'

She stared at him, and then she shook her head. 'No, Liam, I want to know why you won't go into the nursery. I want to know why you haven't been down that end of the house in five years.'

On either side of his plate his hands clenched. He didn't speak. She wasn't sure if he was actually capable of speech at the moment.

She ploughed on. She didn't want to, but for Harry's sake she had to. 'I just told you about one of the worst episodes in my life. I told you because I think you deserve to know why

I can't raise Harry. I need to be honest with you about that. I need to be honest with myself. For Harry's sake. You have to be just as honest—if not with me, then at least with yourself.'

'Or what?' he burst out. 'You'll take Harry away? I'm his last option!'

'No, you're not.' She struggled to keep her voice even. 'There are a lot of couples out there who pray on a daily basis for a child like Harry.'

He paled. 'You'd rather give him to strangers?'

'I'd rather give him to someone I know will love and cherish him!'

They stared at each other, both breathing hard. 'You still don't believe I'll love him,' Liam finally said.

She forced herself to speak the truth as she saw it. 'At the moment, it seems to me he's a duty you need to perform in memory of your brother, to expiate this imagined guilt of yours.' She paused. 'You haven't seemed particularly over-joyed to discover you have a nephew.'

'Look, I'm not a particularly over-joyful kind of guy, all right?'

She could see that about him. It made her sad.

'You haven't gone out of your way to make friends with him either.' That had all been down to her. 'At times you even seem scared of him.'

'I bought him Moo-Moo! I fed him this evening, didn't I?'

And he had sung. She couldn't forget that. She clung to it like a talisman.

Neither one of them spoke for a moment.

'Liam, you have to love a child with all of yourself. You can't hold back. That's not how it works.'

'How *does* it work, then?' he shot at her.

'I don't know. But I do know that Harry doesn't deserve a half-hearted commitment. He's a baby. He's innocent. He deserves the best of everything.'

Liam stared at her. His knuckles turned white. 'That

nursery,' he growled. 'It reminds me of the dreams I had as a younger man. Dreams I've long since given up on.'

Her heart burned for him.

'It reminds me of all the ways I've failed.' He dragged a hand down his face, his fingers no longer clenched. 'But you're right. None of that is Harry's fault. He doesn't deserve to pay for my mistakes.'

'Oh, Liam...' To have had so much optimism and hope, and now to have none. 'What happened?'

For a long moment he didn't speak. If he didn't want to talk about it, she wouldn't push. She didn't have the heart for that. Not now.

'When Belinda and I married, I felt like we were on top of the world.' He gave a harsh laugh. 'The arrogance of youth, huh? But we were young, fit and healthy—in our prime. It felt like we had the whole world at our feet.' He was quiet again for a moment. 'We met at the biggest race meeting in the Kimberley calendar. She was visiting relatives. We hit it off straight away.'

Belinda—such a pretty, innocuous name. But one glance into his face told her whatever Belinda had done to him it hadn't been pretty or innocuous. 'So, a whirlwind courtship, then?'

His lips twisted. 'Marry in haste...'

Repent at leisure—the words throbbed in the silence between them.

'I was twenty-four, she was twenty-five. We wanted to start a family straight away. We weren't too concerned when it didn't happen in the first year. But after five years...'

Her breath caught. 'Oh, Liam, I'm sorry.' She knew from all Anna and Jared had gone through how hard that could be.

'The doctors couldn't find any reason for it. Belinda became angry, withdrawn...bitter. She started spending less time at Newarra and more time at our unit in Perth.'

His shoulders slumped. 'I did everything I could think of to try and reassure her—but it seemed nothing was good enough. *I* wasn't good enough. In the end family and friends advised me to give her some time and space. There didn't seem to be anything else to do, so I threw myself into work.'

His eyes had gone dark. She wanted to reach out and touch his hand, only she didn't think he'd welcome the comfort.

'And then one day she came home. It'd been five months since I'd clapped eyes on her, but she seemed calmer, more at peace. She told me she was sorry.' He paused. 'She told me she still loved me, and I believed her.'

Sapphie had to close her eyes at the bitterness that laced those words. 'What happened?'

'She fell pregnant. Just like that. It seemed too good to be true—a miracle.' He speared her with those blue eyes of his. 'It *was* too good to be true. Can you see where I'm going with this, Sapphie?'

'The baby…it wasn't yours?' she whispered.

'A fact that became all too apparent when the real father showed up at the hospital. He read the birth announcement in the paper and did the math.'

Sapphie pressed a hand to her chest. 'Oh, Liam!'

'We had paternity tests done that confirmed the child wasn't mine.'

'But she returned to you. She wanted to be with you. That must've counted for something.'

He sat back, his mouth twisting. 'It turned out that all Belinda had ever really wanted was my money, and the status the Stapleton family would give her. She'd thought that by providing me with an heir it would guarantee her right to the first and her place in the second. By the time she'd worked out how wrong she was it was too late.'

Sapphie's heart burned. Her throat burned. She could tell by his clenched fists, closed face, the darkness in his eyes, how much Belinda's betrayal had torn him apart, how much it had disillusioned him. Belinda had betrayed him in every way possible.

'But I'd learned my lesson.'

Her heart stuttered in her chest. 'What lesson is that?'

'That I will never remarry. Lachlan and Lacey's children can continue the family name…and now Lucas's child.'

He reached across and covered her hand with his own. 'But you're right, Sapphie. None of this is Harry's fault, and he doesn't deserve to pay for it.'

She swallowed and nodded, aware of the calluses that lined his fingers, how rough they felt against her skin…and how exciting.

'I want you to know that I have heard what you've been trying to say.'

'Okay,' she whispered.

He searched her face, and then in one abrupt movement he pushed away from the table—away from her. 'It's been a long day. I'm off to bed. Goodnight.'

She did her best to not notice his lean hips, the latent power in his long legs as he strode from the room. She tried to erase from her mind the memory of his body's hard strength when he'd helped her hobble to the steps yesterday. She curled her hand—the one he'd covered with his own—inside her other hand and held it to her chest.

There was no future for her and Liam—none at all. But there might just be one for Harry and Liam. She had to focus all her energies on that.

Liam and Harry. It *could* work.

A man who'd wanted children so badly, who'd tried so hard to have them…

She recalled the look in his eye, and fear suddenly prickled across her skin. If Liam ever found out about her, about the abortion she'd had when she was eighteen, he'd do everything in his power to prevent her from ever clapping eyes on Harry again.

She tried to swallow back her fear. Told herself to stop being silly. She hadn't told a single soul about that abortion.

The only way Liam would find out would be if she told him herself. And that was about as likely as either one of them sprouting feathers and learning to fly.

CHAPTER SEVEN

SAPPHIE didn't see much of Liam the next day. Oh, he helped feed Harry at mealtimes, but he disappeared immediately afterwards. He didn't volunteer to help settle Harry for the night. He didn't enter the nursery.

She gave him his space. By the day after that, though, she'd had enough. Liam might need time and space to adjust to Harry's arrival, to deal with all the things he'd revealed about his marriage, but they only had a fortnight. Her heart ached for him. But it ached for Harry too.

In the last seven years she'd done her level best to bury every maternal instinct that had risen in her, but she found now she'd do anything if it meant securing Harry's happiness.

'You know what, Harry?' she said, as she finished cleaning the kitchen after breakfast. 'I think it's time we explored further afield.' They hadn't ventured beyond the perimeter of the garden so far. 'What do you think?'

'Sapph! Sapph! Sapph!'

Sapphie swung round, stared at where Harry sat on the floor with his blocks. 'Harry, boy—what did you say?' She must have misheard. She must have…

'Sapph! Sapph! Sapph!' he repeated. And he grinned at her—a wide, gummy grin that lit up his whole face.

Sapphie's legs turned to rubber. She sat. And then she grinned back at him. She suspected it was one of her goofy, foolish numbers, because it made Harry chortle. He crawled over to her, pulled himself up to a standing position and patted her knee.

'Sapph! Sapph! Sapph!'

Her heart soared. 'Clever boy!' She picked him up and buried her face in his neck, relishing his solid weight, the scent of him and his warmth.

And then her heart plummeted. Just like that. Tears suddenly clogged her throat and her eyes. 'Oh, Harry,' she choked out. 'How am I ever going to give you up?'

You gave up one baby. You can give up another.

She had to bite her lip to stop from crying out. With all her heart she wanted this—a baby, a family, Harry. One bad decision had denied her that for ever. And she couldn't go back and put it to rights. There was nothing she could do to make amends. Ever.

She forced the tears back. Harry was all that mattered here. Not her. And being with Liam was what would be best for him.

So just get on with it.

'Hey, Harry.' She stood. 'Let's go find Uncle Liam and see where he hangs out, shall we? Let's find out what he does all day.'

''Orse!' Harry demanded as she started for the door.

'Silly me!'

She wheeled back to sweep Horsie up from the floor, the excess material of her shirt nearly tripping her up as she rose again. 'Rotten thing.' She'd constantly had to pull the sleeves up as she'd cleaned. Whenever she set Harry down or picked him up he got caught or tangled in it.

So why was she wearing it?

She stilled. She glanced around the kitchen, out of the window. She had nothing to fear out here. She bit her lip. She set Harry down.

She took it off.

Her heart hammered. She smoothed down the T-shirt she

wore beneath it, tucked it into her jeans. And then she remembered the heat in Liam's eyes when they'd rested on her the other night, the answering heat that had surged through her. She might want to breathe a little more freely, but not *that* freely.

Slowly she pulled the shirt back on. At the last minute she left the top two buttons undone and rolled up the sleeves. There—that was better. Not brilliant, but better.

She and Harry sallied forth. Once past the hedge of plumbago at the edge of the lawn the landscape changed—to red earth, yellow rock and pale native grasses. The air smelt dry and clean, and Sapphie filled her lungs with it, throwing her head back to stare at the unending blue above her—the same blue as Liam's eyes. She felt at home out here in the vast wildness in a way she'd always figured she'd had no right to. But if she was Bryce Curran's daughter then perhaps the love of this land was in her blood?

She didn't want to think about Bryce today.

Well, when, then?

Some other time.

She stared at the various outbuildings that arced out from the house. 'That's probably the head stockman's cottage,' she said, pointing it out to Harry. 'And that'll be the ringers' quarters. Ooh, a huge machinery shed. That there's a cattle yard, though it's not a big one. Umm…and a barn and probably stables.'

Harry regarded her solemnly. She grinned. 'I bet you'd love the stables.' He grinned back, and that settled it.

As they approached the huge double doors of the barn, Liam rode out from the inner shade on a big bay horse. Its hooves clattered against the hard ground at a slow canter. He brought it to a halt the moment he saw Sapphie and Harry.

Harry stiffened.

Sapphie sighed on one big out-breath. She couldn't help it. Her whole body softened. Liam looked more at home on a horse than he did with both long legs planted firmly on the ground. His movements matched and merged with the movements of his horse with an ease that should have had admiration, not lust, surging through her.

No, no...it wasn't lust. She didn't *do* lust. It *was* admiration.

The horse wheeled around, impatient for a canter, but at an imperceptible tightening of the reins and a low word the horse bowed to its master's command, dropping its head and quietening immediately.

Oh, dear. It wasn't admiration wheeling through her veins. She grew so soft she threatened to melt into a puddle of warm goo.

She opened her mouth, but before something stupid and revealing dropped out of it Harry started bouncing in her arms. "Orse! 'Orse!' he shouted, pointing.

His unguarded excitement took her breath away. 'Is it okay for Harry to pat your horse?' She knew Liam would realise what she was really asking—is it safe?

He stared down at Harry, and his face lost its hard edges. 'Sure it is.'

'Look, Harry.' Sapphie reached out and stroked the horse's neck. She took his hand and placed it on the horse's neck too.

His eyes went wide. ''Orse,' he whispered.

'That's right. This is Uncle Liam's horse, and his name is...?'

'Jasper.' Liam leant down and placed his hand on Jasper's neck, not far from Harry's hand. Not far from Sapphie's. 'Harry, meet Jasper.'

And then Harry did something Sapphie couldn't have predicted in a thousand years. He held his arms up to Liam. ''Orse!' And in that moment she knew Harry and Liam would be fine—they belonged together—and something inside her broke.

This was what she wanted.

It was what she'd been working so hard towards. But that didn't make the pain flooding her heart ease.

'Sapphie?' A frown marred Liam's forehead.

She snapped to, realising he hadn't attempted to take Harry from her. She lifted her chin and stuck out a hip, pretended to eye him up and down. 'You look like you might be a halfway decent rider?'

One corner of his mouth kicked up. 'I can hold my own.'

'And can you hold Harry on the saddle in front of you whilst controlling your horse?'

'Yep.'

She didn't hesitate. She handed Harry up to him. She knew him well enough to know he'd never put Harry at risk. She had to laugh at the child's face when Liam urged his horse forward to walk in a wide circle around Sapphie.

She clapped her hands. Harry squealed and beamed, then leant forward to hug Jasper's mane and kiss him. Liam kept one large hand anchored around Harry's middle. She had to laugh again. 'Oh, Harry.' She clasped her hands under her chin. 'That looks like so much fun.'

'Can you ride?'

She glanced up at Liam. His face had gone all soft again, and who could blame him? To see the trauma start to fade from Harry's face and mind, to see him happy and excited… She couldn't remember a more bittersweet moment in her entire life—knowing Harry would be safe and happy, loved and looked after, and yet knowing that in a fundamental way she'd just lost him.

She couldn't keep him.

No, she couldn't.

She did her best to smile. 'Yeah, I can ride. But it's been a while. And I wouldn't trust myself to do that.' She waved to the way he held Harry in front of him.

'Hey, Rob?' Liam called out.

A ringer, probably a couple of years younger than Sapphie, appeared in the barn's doorway. 'Yeah, boss?'

'Saddle up Miss Lil for Ms Thomas here.'

'Sure thing.' Rob touched the brim of his hat in Sapphie's

direction and disappeared. He emerged a few minutes later with a grey mare.

'Oh!' Sapphie gasped. 'She's beautiful.'

'Do you need a leg-up?' Liam asked.

She lifted her nose in the air. 'Absolutely not.'

He grinned, and she swore it lifted her all the way up into the saddle. She adjusted the length of the stirrups and beamed around at the world. She had a feeling her excitement was as transparent as Harry's, because something had made Liam chuckle and he was looking straight at her when he did it. It made her go warm all over.

No, no, that was the sun.

'I love to ride,' she confided. 'But I don't get a chance to do much of it in Perth.'

'You have a good seat.'

Man! The sun must be nearing meltdown capacity. She glanced skywards. She managed to not fan her face—just.

'Too right,' Liam muttered, urging his horse inside the barn. He re-emerged a moment later, carrying, in addition to Harry, two Akubra hats.

He handed one to Sapphie. She plonked it on her head immediately, welcoming the shade it gave her. By Kimberley standards it wasn't hot—it would be winter in a couple of weeks, though really the only acknowledged seasons out here were wet and dry. Regardless of the season, it didn't lessen the glare of the sun.

She had to chuckle when Liam placed the other hat on Harry's head. It was tiny!

'We all had these as babies,' Liam explained. 'Dad had them specially made. I hunted out my old one the other day, and dusted it off for Harry.'

His hat, not Lucas's. She wondered if her face had gone as soft as her insides. She adjusted her hat's brim and hoped it hid the expression in her eyes. 'That was thoughtful of you.'

'Need a hat out here,' was all he said.

'Uh huh.' She wanted to say a whole lot more, but she bit her tongue.

With a shrug, Liam turned his horse away from the barn and out towards the open landscape. 'We'll take a ride down to the creek. Harry can splash around for a bit if he wants.'

They didn't ride along exactly in silence. Harry chatted away to her, to Liam, to Jasper. It was as if a switch had been flicked on inside him—as if the sight of Liam's big bay horse had made the world right for him.

She was glad for him. *She was*, she told herself fiercely. She stared about her, determined to enjoy their ride, determined to drink in the scenery.

In the distance a sandstone and granite range rose out of the plain, the orange of the sandstone brilliant in the late-morning sun. Stretching to the base of the range was low scrub, spiky native grasses and, beneath it all, red dirt. Liam edged them to the left, towards two boab trees. As a kid she'd called them upside down trees, because of their peculiar shape. Even now they made her smile.

Sapphie wasn't sure for how long they rode—twenty minutes, perhaps—before she and Miss Lil followed Liam, Harry and Jasper down a shallow gully that wound around and then opened out to reveal the creek.

'Oh, how lovely!' The words burst from her. Harry clapped his hands.

In the wet season the creek would be a gushing torrent, but now, in the dry, it was placid and shallow. Wide rock shelves surrounded clear pools and a sense of peace invaded her soul.

She dismounted and, at Liam's command, left her horse to graze at will. Then she took Harry, so Liam could dismount as well. When he reached the ground he took Harry back in his arms as if it were the most natural thing in the world. She had to bite her lip to stop from crying out; had to remind herself that this was what was best for Harry.

She sat cross-legged on a rock shelf and watched Harry and

Liam frolic in a shady rock pool. Liam had removed his boots and socks, rolled up his jeans, and divested Harry of his playsuit and nappy. Harry kicked and splashed, soaking them both.

They had such fun. Liam was enjoying this moment with his little nephew with such unguarded relish that before too long Sapphie had to laugh—enjoying it by proxy. She'd known from the very beginning that letting Harry go would be hard, but look what she was letting him go to—a wonderful home, a wonderful life, and a man who would love him unconditionally.

Harry couldn't ask for more.

Finally Liam glanced up and speared her with the intense blue of his eyes, and she suddenly found the brim of her hat no shelter from him at all. 'You want to tell me what happened back there?'

She stiffened. 'Back where?'

'Back in the yard? When Harry held his arms out to me?'

She rolled her shoulders, tossed her head. 'I have no idea what you're talking about.'

'We're going to talk about it, Sapphie, because you looked like the world had come to an end.'

Her jaw dropped. 'You don't pull your punches, do you?'

'You weren't exactly holding them back at dinner the other night when you were asking about my wife, either.'

Touché. She moistened suddenly dry lips. 'What Belinda did, Liam—I'm sorry. It must've been awful.'

Liam wanted to close his eyes and ignore her words, but there was no mistaking Sapphie's sincerity. Besides, if he closed his eyes now it would give her the right to do exactly the same.

He didn't want her closing her eyes. He wanted to get to the bottom of whatever had hurt her.

'Thank you,' he mumbled instead.

'I saw my sister and her husband go through the hell that

is IVF—without a happy ending. It nearly destroyed them. I don't know if it's any consolation at all, but what Belinda did…she would've been in a dark place. I doubt she did it out of malice.'

His chest tightened. 'You can't know that.'

Her arms went about her knees, pulling them in close to her chest. He suddenly noticed her sleeves were pushed up, and the skin on her forearms was pale and…pretty.

Harry chose that moment to splash him. Under his breath, Liam thanked him. He didn't *want* to notice the pale perfection of Sapphie's skin, or the creamy line of her throat. He sure as heck didn't want to wonder if it would be as soft to the touch as it looked.

'Desperation can drive people to do terrible things.'

Her words hauled him back.

'I know you think you were completely mistaken about her, but I can't imagine you marrying someone who was totally devoid of compassion and goodness and…' she reached into the air as if to pluck a word from it '…love. You don't strike me as completely stupid.'

He found one corner of his mouth loosening and hitching upwards at that. He couldn't explain why, but the tightness in his chest had started to ease. 'But?'

'You must've had some fun together. There must've been some good times.'

'Yeah, maybe. But after what happened those good times don't seem to hold much value.' His marriage had been a lie from start to finish.

Or had it?

He eased back. In the early days, before the fear that they couldn't have children, their life had seemed almost perfect. After that, though, had come Belinda's panic, the frantic round of specialists' appointments…her increasing desperation. He'd tried telling her that it didn't matter if she never fell pregnant, but he hadn't been able to deny he'd wanted kids with a fierceness that had taken him off guard. Even so, he would never have deserted Belinda to have a child with someone else. He could never condone what she had done— she'd torn both of their lives apart—but for the first time the faintest glimmer of understanding threaded through him.

'I never looked at it like that before,' he said slowly, gruffly. He didn't want to say anything else. He wasn't used to talking about this stuff. But then he remembered he wanted her to open up to him, so he unglued his lips and added, 'And perhaps it does help. It might be a…' what was the word she'd used? '…a consolation.'

Sapphie eased back to rest her weight on her hands, stretched her legs out in front of her. Her eyes danced. 'Man, you must *really* want to know why I looked so gloomy earlier, huh?'

She'd seen right through him!

He tore his gaze from the long, luscious lines of her to splash water onto Harry's chest. Harry ignored him, intent on trying to grasp the smooth pebbles that lay on the bottom of the pool. Liam kept one hand firmly anchored around him. 'Yeah, I do.'

The brim of her hat hid the precise green of her eyes, but it didn't hide the shadows that chased themselves across her face. 'Might I ask why?'

He kept his gaze steady. 'Because I need to know if it's going to impact on me and Harry.'

She ducked her head, and all he could see was the crown of her hat, not her face. *And to make sure that you'll be okay.* But he couldn't say those words out loud. He did his best to harden his heart. 'Sapphie?'

She lifted her head and smiled. Not an ounce of sadness or care darkened her face, but he sensed it shivering beneath the surface.

'When Harry lifted his arms to go to you,' she started, 'it was the first real indication that he will be fine here with you.'

He tried not to frown. 'That made you sad?'

'No.'

She moistened her lips. He wished he didn't notice their shine, or the sweet fullness of her bottom lip.

'What made me sad was the realisation that soon Harry won't need me at all.'

She hadn't just been sad. She'd been stricken. The look on her face had torn at him.

'Now, before you say anything, I know Harry has been too dependent on me, and I know we've been working hard towards him forging a connection with you, and I know all this is in his best interests. But—' she glared '—it doesn't mean it isn't hard or that I have to be overjoyed about it all the time. All right?'

During her fierce little speech he'd dangled his free hand in the water. He lifted it now, and dragged it down his face, but the cool wetness did nothing to ease the pounding at his temples.

Sapphie loved Harry. She just didn't believe she could have him.

Because of Emmy? Because she thought she'd ruined Emmy's life?

'Even if I could have Harry, Liam, I can't give him what you can.' She stood and spread her arms out to encompass their surroundings. 'I can't give him this wonderful station to grow up on, or the kind of financial security you can.'

'There's more to bringing up a child than money,' he snapped.

'Yeah, well, you try bringing one up without any!'

She planted her hands on her hips. Beneath her shirt—*shirts*, he amended—her breasts rose and fell. He dragged his gaze back to her face and gritted his teeth.

'Are you telling me you can't love Harry as much or as deeply as me?' she demanded.

'No.' The last half-hour had taught him that. He glanced down at his nephew and a fierce surge of protectiveness engulfed him…and something strong and clean and pure—love?

'Do you believe you can love Harry like your own child?

As well and as deeply as the children you wished you could've had with Belinda?'

It hit him—the knowledge, the realisation—just like that. 'Yes.' The word rang loud in the clear air. And then he remembered something Sapphie said to him. *Harry is not a replacement for Lucas.*

A replacement? He frowned. No… His mouth went dry. From the very first moment he'd held his nephew all he'd focussed on was what he'd get if Harry stayed: the healing of his own wounds and those of the rest of his family. What he *should* have been thinking about was Harry—what was best for him.

He recognised now, with a clarity he'd lacked before, all the reasons behind Sapphie's reservations. Harry *wasn't* a replacement—not for Lucas, and not for the children Liam had never had. Harry was Harry—he was himself. And Liam loved him for it.

He met Sapphie's eyes. 'I couldn't love a natural-born son more than I love Harry.'

The tension left her shoulders.

'Harry is not a replacement or a substitute or an alternative. He's a gift.'

She nodded. 'That's all right, then.'

He stared at her, amazed. He knew she loved Harry as strongly as he did. Could *he* be that generous if their situations were reversed?

He glanced back down at Harry, to find his nephew surveying him. Harry gurgled and smiled. A thrill shot through Liam's entire body. Here was Harry, with his chubby cheeks and his big baby smile and his wonder, and it was all directed at him. *At him.*

He knew he'd fight any fight to keep Harry now. Harry was a part of him. Harry was a miracle—a second chance, his family.

As if she'd read his mind, Sapphie said, 'You can give him something far more important than financial security.'

'What's that?'

'A family. A big, lively, loving family who will embrace him and support him and love him. That has to be worth its weight in gold.'

She was right. And it was a family, he suddenly realised, that he'd neglected since Lucas's death. He'd thrown himself into the running of the station, hiding away with his guilt and his regret. His parents hadn't lost one son, but two.

He dragged that hand down his face again. He stared at Sapphie and tried to imagine how she must feel. 'I don't know how to make this process easier for you,' he finally admitted.

She stumbled, as if his words had knocked her sideways. 'You don't need to worry about me. I'm a big girl. I'll survive. I'm used to taking care of myself. It's Harry we need to make things easy for. I'll just content myself with being his favourite auntie.'

As she spoke, she moved down to where he and Harry sat. He lifted Harry out of the water, balanced him on his hip, uncaring about the wetness that soaked into his shirt. He hooked his other arm around Sapphie's shoulders and drew her in close for a hug. For one brief moment she sank against him, as if she'd like nothing more than to rest her head on his shoulder, and for that brief moment the world felt strangely right and complete. But then she stiffened and pulled away.

'What was that for?'

'I think you're one of the most courageous women I know.'

'Don't be ridiculous!' She raked him up and down with a glare. 'I think you've had too much sun. C'mon—if you and your men are hoping to get lunch today, then it's time we made tracks.'

CHAPTER EIGHT

LIAM pushed his plate away and patted his stomach. 'They were great—thanks, Sapphie.'

She'd made sandwiches for lunch—doorstop slabs of bread and thick slices of roast beef with a generous slathering of pickles. Now she cut a fat slice of sultana cake and set it in front of him, before putting the jug on to boil and making a pot of tea.

He took a bite. 'The men will enjoy this.' It was one of the ringers' duties to cook breakfast and dinner for the men, but the homestead provided lunch. Sapphie had the knack of knowing what would satisfy a man's hunger *and* keep him going for an afternoon of hard work.

'Dana's recipe. Again. She taught me them all.'

And he was looking forward to sampling the lot. Mention of Dana, though, had him thinking about the rest of Sapphie's family. He knew so little about her—except that she was brave and generous. And that she loved Harry.

'Tell me about your other sister. The one who was on IVF.' He'd earlier formed the impression that Emmy was her only sibling.

She spun round and turned so deathly pale he shot to his feet and reached for her, his hands curving around her upper arms as he led her to a chair and urged her to sit.

'Sorry,' she mumbled. 'I must've had a touch too much sun today.'

'You're a rotten liar.' He pushed a glass of water into her hand. 'Drink.' Wouldn't she *ever* trust him?

She eyed him warily. He crouched down in front of her. 'You demand to know all *my* history, but you won't tell me anything of yours?'

Sure, she'd told him why she couldn't raise Harry, but she still hadn't told him why Emmy wanted to relinquish Harry. He was sensible enough not to push her on that front, though. He'd wait until she was ready to tell him.

'I'm not the one being vetted to see if I'll make a good mother to Harry.'

She'd make a great mother. The best. She was young, lovely. She'd meet someone and have children of her own eventually. He didn't know why, but the notion burned a path of resentment through him. Stupid! He wasn't interested in travelling down *that* particular path again.

Sapphie would never betray a man the way Belinda had betrayed him.

He tried to shrug the thought off. It didn't make a jot of difference.

Suddenly, though, he wasn't so sure. He forced himself back to his own chair. It was no more than three feet away, but the metaphorical distance seemed vast...and Sapphie looked so lost and alone. 'You don't need to prove yourself, Sapphie. Not to me, not to anyone. But there are other reasons for sharing confidences.'

'Like?'

'What about friendship?'

Her eyes softened. 'Oh!' she said. It was all she said.

He tried again. Gently. 'I thought Emmy was your only sister?'

She pulled in a breath that made her whole frame shudder. 'So did I.'

She stared at him for what seemed like an eternity. He wondered if he'd measure up. He wanted to measure up.

'You ever have one of those days that changes your whole life?' she whispered.

'I've had a couple.' The tension inside him started to ease. He found he could even smile after a fashion. 'The most recent being the day a rather determined woman jumped out of the mail plane and presented me with my nephew.'

That made her smile too. 'Mine came a couple of days earlier than that—on my twenty-fifth birthday.'

'When you were landed with Harry?'

'The same day I received a letter from my mother.'

'But she's...'

'Yeah, I know.' She glanced down at her hands. 'She'd left instructions with her solicitor that a letter be delivered to me the day I turned twenty-five.'

'What did it say?'

She lifted a shoulder, gave a funny little smile that tore at his heart. 'That Bryce Curran was my biological father.'

His jaw dropped. He hauled it back up and let loose with a whistle. 'That's some clanger, Sapphie.' He made the next leap. 'So Lea and Anna Curran—they're...'

'My half-sisters,' she whispered.

He sat back and stared. 'Why all the secrecy?' he finally asked. To find out all this, on top of Harry...

'I was conceived when Bryce's wife was still alive.'

Liam had heard about Karen Curran's long, drawn-out illness. He also knew how much Bryce had reportedly loved his wife. And yet he'd...

He shook the thought off. 'That might explain why he didn't come forward when you were a baby, but what about later?'

'I don't really know.' He watched her swallow and his hands clenched. 'I think he thought it would hurt Anna and Lea too much.'

What about Sapphie? Who'd been thinking about Sapphie? Taking care of her needs? Providing for her wants?

'And what do you think?' he demanded.

She shrugged, as if what she thought didn't matter. His gut tightened. It mattered all right!

She lifted her chin. 'I would never do anything to hurt Anna or Lea.'

Hurt them? If Anna and Lea had half the heart of the woman in front of him they'd be overjoyed to discover she was their half-sister. He leant forward, intent and earnest. 'Sapphie, you have to tell them the truth.' He sensed how much she loved them. 'You told me they're your best friends.' Loneliness stretched across her face and he had to fight the urge to pull her into his arms. 'They love you too, you know?'

'It's one thing to be someone's best friend. It's an altogether different thing to discover she's your half-sister.'

She was afraid that in Anna and Lea's eyes she wouldn't measure up. That was crazy nonsense! He'd only met the Curran girls a couple of times. They were closer in age to Lacey than to him, but he was sure Sapphie was wrong.

'Are Anna and Lea preoccupied with money and status?' he demanded. Jarndirri was a huge station, worth millions.

She glared at him. 'Of course they're not!'

'Do they have that streak of meanness in them that some people have? Do they hold a grudge? Can they be spiteful? Are they—?'

'Get over yourself, Liam! They're my *friends*!' She shot to her feet, her hands clenched into fists. He tried not to grin. 'They work hard for everything they've got. They're loyal and kind. They'd never do anyone a bad turn and they're great to have around in an emergency. What's more, they're smart and funny and the world is a whole lot better off for having them in it!'

'Exactly.'

He watched as realisation dawned in her glorious green eyes. 'Oh.' She dropped back into her chair.

'Sapphie, you've been given a gift. I had a brother who died. Losing him was hell. But I had twenty-three years with him. I wouldn't swap that for anything.'

'Lucas?' she whispered.

'Lucas,' he agreed.

He leant forward. She was only a fingertip away. 'Promise me that when you leave here you'll arrange to meet Anna and Lea and that you'll tell them the truth. They deserve to know. They deserve the chance to love you like a sister.'

Her eyes filled with tears, but they didn't spill onto her cheeks. She smiled, clasped her hands beneath her chin, and he'd never seen anyone look more truly lovely. 'I will if you promise me something in return.'

'What?' He almost added, *anything*, but he remembered himself in time.

'I'll talk to Anna and Lea if you promise to invite your entire family to Newarra for Christmas this year.'

He sat back. 'I…' Last Christmas had been awful. Awful because Lucas had been gone…awful because the family hadn't had the heart to gather together.

Or because he hadn't been able to bear the thought of holding the traditional family Christmas?

He thought about it. Slowly he nodded. 'Deal.'

That night, Liam fed Harry his tin of chocolate custard. Sapphie watched him out of the corner of her eyes whilst she prepared Harry's bottle. When he'd finished, he rose, dropped the empty tin into the kitchen bin and left the kitchen.

Without a word. As he'd done every night so far this week.

Sapphie bit back a sigh. He still hadn't volunteered to help put Harry down for the night. He still avoided the nursery.

She couldn't push him. The final decision rested with him. But if he couldn't overcome that particular hurdle…

She glanced at Harry and her chest started to cramp.

'I…uh…'

She spun around to find Liam standing in the doorway, *holding his guitar!* She held her breath.

'I…uh…thought…' He started again. 'If it's all right with

you and Harry, I could play the guitar for him when you put him down for the night?'

It was more than all right! She did her best to temper her excitement. Liam would not welcome the fuss. 'Of course it is.' She kept her voice brusque, as if he made the offer every other day. But she suspected her smile threatened to split her face in two. 'What do you say, Harry?'

Harry gurgled and lifted up his arms.

Sapphie led the way to the nursery, almost preternaturally aware of the man behind her—of his heat and his lean promise. The blood in her veins thickened, making her movements slow and clumsy, making her feel as if she were wading through warm honey.

They entered the nursery. She wanted to cast a glance behind her, to make sure Liam was okay, but she forced herself forward, forced herself to keep this normal…or at least as normal as she could.

She settled Harry in his cot with his bottle. Only then did she glance across at Liam. He hovered in the doorway in all his heart-stopping, heat-inducing male glory, but beneath those broad shoulders she sensed his awkwardness. The vision of the queen-sized bed in the adjoining room hit her.

What would it be like to make love to this man? Excitement, not fear, rushed through her at the thought.

She gulped and waved him to the sofa. She stayed by the cot, leaning down to coo at Harry. Looking at Harry meant she didn't have to look at Liam.

Talking to Harry was easier than talking to Liam too. 'Uncle Liam is going to play us a song. A quiet song,' she added quickly.

'"Fernando"?'

She had to glance up at that. 'What's *your* favourite music, Liam? Maybe you should create your own traditions and history with Harry?'

He paused. 'This was one of Lucas's favourite songs,' he finally said.

He played a slow, sweet song, a beautiful song, and an ache as big as the Kimberley opened in Sapphie's chest. She remained beside Harry's cot, but her heart followed every lift and dip of the melody that Liam played.

'That was lovely,' she whispered, when it came to an end.

The only light in the room came from a lamp by the door, and the play of shadows on Liam's face gave him an other-worldly look. He could be a devil…or an angel.

Stop being fanciful, she chided. He was a flesh-and-blood man.

Hot-blooded and firm-fleshed.

For heaven's sake, she had to get her mind off that!

'Come over and sit here with me.'

She gulped. 'But Harry's eyes are still open.'

'Sapphie?' He held out his hand to her, a devil or an angel sent to tempt her.

She did as he asked. She told herself she didn't really want to, but that was a lie. She wanted to do a whole lot more than just sit beside him. But she couldn't afford to be quite that candid.

Not with the lights so dim.

Not when such romantic music poured from Liam's fingertips. She wasn't ready for that.

She nodded towards Harry. 'You think I'm fussing, don't you?'

He raised an eyebrow.

'Maybe I am. But…but I want to protect him from everything that might hurt him.'

His fingers closed around hers, squeezed gently. 'I know. But there's nothing in this room that can hurt him.'

She knew what he was saying—that he'd protect Harry with his last breath if he had to, that he'd never hurt him. And she believed him. The silence between them stretched. He still held her hand.

She gulped and tugged it free. 'Play another song,' she

whispered, not wanting to give the heat building through her a chance to ignite.

He did. She didn't recognise the song, but it soothed her.

When he'd finished, he rose and went to the cot. Sapphie had to grip her hands together to fight the over-protective urge to join him there. He turned with a finger to his lips, then pointed to the door. She nodded and followed him out.

Neither one of them so much as glanced at the queen-sized bed as they passed it.

When they reached the kitchen, Liam snagged Sapphie's hand and swung her around to face him. 'Sapphie, thank you.'

Relief poured through him. Relief that he'd been able to enter the nursery and stay there. Relief that failure and misery hadn't swamped him. Relief that he could do it after all—be a good and proper father to Harry.

Her eyes went wide. 'For what?'

'For not pushing. For making it all as easy for me as you could.'

'Did you think I wouldn't?'

It suddenly hit him that that was exactly what he'd thought. But Sapphie wasn't Belinda. She wasn't like any woman he'd ever met.

And he owed her so much!

Gratitude welled through him, mixing with his relief and bubbling up into a heady sense of optimism. Before he could think better of it, he leant forward and kissed her.

He hadn't meant to let his lips linger on hers. If he'd been thinking straight he wouldn't have kissed her in the first place. The kiss was meant to be a thank-you—a brief touch of his lips to hers—a symbol of his gratitude.

The moment his lips met hers, though, all those intentions flew out of his head. Their lips met and some frozen thing inside him started to melt. Warmth flooded his whole body.

It happened in an eye-blink.

Sapphie gasped, her mouth opening in surprise, and he couldn't resist touching his tongue to her inner lips and exploring her soft sweetness. She swayed, and he slid his arm around her waist to hold her close.

And then she froze.

He did too.

Did she want him to stop? He prayed to God she didn't. She started to draw away…loosened his hold…

But then very tentatively, she moved her lips against his—so slowly that the frozen thing inside him thawed completely, sending tenderness spiralling through him. With a tiny sigh she moved in close again. Her head fell back and her hands bunched in the material of his shirt. He tasted her slowly, thoroughly, wanting—needing—to draw a response from her. His fingers curved around her jaw, stroking the soft firm line of her throat, savouring every taste and breath and feel of her. When she touched her tongue to his he was lost.

His hands followed the dip and swell of her back and hips—skimming, teasing and tempting, savouring every discovery. Sapphie's hands curled into his hair and she arched against him, opening herself up more fully for his kisses, his caresses, her gasps driving him on.

He'd never wanted a woman with this intensity before.

He wanted to imprint himself on her, body and soul. He wanted her branded on him, body and soul. *Now!* The physicality of it took him off-guard. Need, desire, heat pounded through him with elemental force. He hadn't experienced anything as primitive or desperate in his life, not even with Belinda, and—

Belinda?

The word pounded in his brain.

Belinda!

With a curse he dragged his mouth from Sapphie's. He

kept hold of her upper arms until she regained her balance, and then he dragged his hands away too. The blood pounded in his ears in time with his breathing—ragged and rapid.

Had he ruined everything?

'I'm sorry.' The words scraped out of him. 'That was supposed to be a thank-you, but it got out of hand.'

She touched her fingers to her lips. Their fullness, their shine, beckoned to him even now, and he could have groaned out loud. She stared at him with big, dazed eyes, and it occurred to him that maybe he *hadn't* offended her. But instead maybe she'd fill her head with all sorts of romantic notions and castles-in-the-air nonsense about him. His skin started to burn and itch. Somehow this woman had got under his skin in a record amount of time.

'It won't happen again.' He wasn't the kind of man a woman should pin her romantic hopes on. He stabbed a finger at her. 'It *can't* happen again!'

She blinked at his ferocity. She didn't say a word. Couldn't she at least agree with him?

'I will not be accused of seducing you to gain access to my nephew.'

That put the starch back into her spine. 'You think too much of yourself, Liam Stapleton. The kiss was all right, but it wasn't that good.'

All right? *All right!* It had blown his mind, but it had obviously left her—

The thought came to a screaming halt as he watched the blood drain from her face. She took a step back. She pressed her hands to her face. And then she turned and fled, through the living room and out of the French doors to the veranda.

What on earth…?

Liam followed more slowly. His gut churned. Would she demand he fly her and Harry out of Newarra? Had he made a hash of everything because of one little kiss?

It hadn't been little, though, had it? Sapphie could pretend, but he sensed it had rocked her as much as it had him. The way she'd just fled proved it.

That darn look—the end of the world look—had come into her eyes again. His hands clenched. He needed to find out why.

He found her huddled on the bench. He cleared his throat to let her know he was there. She stiffened and half turned, but she didn't meet his eyes. 'I think we ought to talk about that,' he said.

'There's nothing to talk about. Other than the fact it can't happen again!'

Coming from her, those words didn't sound half as logical as when *he'd* uttered them. When he looked at her all he wanted to do was kiss her again. He forced himself to stare out towards the pepper trees.

The evening shadows had reached their zenith. The air was blue and still. In another half-hour night would have fallen completely.

He shoved his hands in his pockets. 'You're right. It can't.'

She turned, her eyes narrowed. 'Tell me why?'

He wondered if this was some kind of test. If so, he prayed he'd pass. 'Because I have no intention of ever marrying again, and you don't strike me as the kind of woman who has affairs.'

'You're right about that.'

Bitterness laced her words. It seemed so out of character it made him pause. 'If I kissed you again I'd be leading you on. I have no intention of doing that, Sapphie.'

'Why not?' Again that narrow-eyed stare.

'Because I like you.'

Her jaw dropped. The stiffness slid out of her. It almost made him smile.

That desire fled when he registered the misery on her face. That look tore at him. He hated it. She had a mouth made for laughing and eyes made for smiling, and that was what he wanted for her. The way she wanted good things for him and Harry.

Keeping his movements deliberately casual, he settled himself at one end of the bench. She scooted away until she was jammed up against the far armrest. Her eyes skittered away. He rested his elbows on his knees and stared directly out to the front. He didn't want her feeling as if she was under threat, under attack…or under a microscope.

'Did I frighten you just then?' *The way the blood had drained from her face!* Silently he cursed himself. 'I'm sorry. I—'

'No, you didn't frighten me, Liam. I frightened myself. I… It took me by surprise.'

That made two of them.

'I was so abandoned, so out of control.'

Round eyes and a trembling mouth told him how much that had appalled her.

'If you hadn't stopped when you did…'

'But I did.' He needed to erase that expression from her eyes. 'I swear to you, Sapphie, it won't happen again.'

Her mouth stopped trembling. 'I do believe you, Liam.'

His stomach tightened. 'But?' He could sense one coming.

'It's just…' She pulled her knees up and wrapped her arms around them. 'It's just that I never thought I'd feel desire for a man again.'

Everything inside him stilled. It took a concerted effort to keep his hands relaxed, his voice even. 'Why not?'

As if she suddenly realised she'd said too much, she stiffened. 'It's a long story.' She placed her feet back on the floor and made as if to rise.

'I'd like to hear it.'

She pursed her lips, then wrinkled her nose. 'I don't want you feeling sorry for me.'

One of his hands curled into a fist. 'I promise not to feel sorry for you.'

She slumped back against the bench, as if the fight had left her body. 'I guess it's not really a secret,' she mumbled.

What wasn't?

'I just don't talk about it all that often.'

He wanted her to talk about it now.

She drew in a deep breath. 'When I was eighteen I was raped by a family friend. It wasn't long after my mother had died, and at first I thought he was trying to comfort me.' She shrugged. 'It was awful.'

He couldn't have clenched his hands tighter if he'd tried. His muscles had tensed to hard knots and his whole body shook.

Sapphie glanced at him and gave a low laugh. 'Ease up, Liam. He died a few years ago—heart attack.'

Liam could barely unclench his teeth to ask, 'Was he charged with what he did to you?'

She stared down at her hands. 'There wasn't enough evidence, apparently.'

Not enough…?

He leapt up and paced. 'But that's—'

'Unfair? Yeah, I know.'

He stared at her. How had she managed to get through such an ordeal *on her own*?

'The rape itself wasn't particularly violent. He didn't hit me or beat me. He just…overpowered me.' Her lips twisted, but he saw the pain she tried to hide. 'And…' She swallowed. 'Emmy was in the house.'

Bile rose through him when he saw her remembered helplessness, her fear. She met his gaze and her eyes almost seem to plead with his for understanding.

'I didn't want Emmy to hear,' she whispered. 'I didn't want him to hurt *her*. She'd been through so much…'

So had Sapphie! But he understood her urge to protect her younger sibling.

'So in the end there weren't that many bruises. It was my word against his, and no jury would've convicted him on that.'

He wanted to punch something. But when he glanced at

her he saw how she sat on the bench, so hunched and small, and he had to swallow back the violence roiling through him and go to her.

He covered both her hands with one of his own. 'I'm sorry, Sapphie. That should never have happened to you. It should never happen to anyone.'

He pulled his hand back, conscious that he might be invading her space. Her baggy shirts, those buttoned-up collars—all suddenly made sense. Today, though, for the first time she'd left her top button undone and had rolled up her sleeves. She'd started to feel safe. And he'd jeopardised her sense of safety by kissing her.

'It's okay, Liam.'

She reached across and slipped her hand inside his. He wanted to caress it, stroke it, kiss it. But none of those things would undo what had been done to her.

'I know you're not the kind of man who would ever hurt a woman.'

Something inside him unhitched at her words. No, he would never hurt a woman, and for as long as Sapphie was here at Newarra nobody would hurt *her*. He'd make sure of it.

'Liam?'

He met her glorious green eyes, and only the merest shadow of sadness lingered in them.

'I do understand that most men wouldn't dream of forcing themselves on a woman.'

The anger prickled through him again. 'How can you be so…?'

She pointed the index finger of her free hand at his nose. '*Healthy* is the right word to use.'

It almost made him grin.

'I didn't have time to wallow.'

No, she'd had to look after her twelve-year-old sister.

'I saw a counsellor for a while, but the thing that really helped was taking self-defence classes. It gave me a sense of control again. That and focussing on making a good life with Emmy pulled me through. I was lucky.'

Lucky!

She coloured. 'Until today I thought I'd never want to be…intimate with a man.'

No wonder that kiss had all but winded her. The force of the need that had shot through him had almost knocked him off his feet, and he had nothing like the excuse she did.

She plucked her hand from his. 'I don't mean to do anything about it, though.'

A primitive desire to show her just how good it could be between a man and a woman flared through him. He damped it down. Sapphie was right. It was one thing to recognise and admit to feelings of desire. Taking that next step was something else entirely, and she wasn't ready for it.

Besides, she deserved more than the false hopes he could offer her. The majority of women couldn't cope with the isolation of station life. And even if she proved the exception he was never giving another woman—not even the splendid Sapphie—an opportunity to make a fool of him again.

That knowledge didn't stop him staring at her, marvelling at her.

She lifted a hand to her face. 'What?'

He shook his head. 'In a very short space of time you lost your mother, had to take charge of your twelve-year-old sister, and were raped. And yet…'

'And yet?'

She'd remained buoyant. 'You can still smile and laugh.'

'Of course I can!' She stared at him as if he just didn't get it. 'You know what your problem is? You let all the bad things that happen in your life take away the joy. You forget all the good things.'

No, he didn't. He rolled his shoulders and scowled. He…

'Nobody said life is fair—or easy—but it's still a gift. If you lose your joy then…then it's won.'

'What's won?'

'The badness.'

With that she stood and disappeared back inside the house. Left him wondering if she was right—*was* he letting the bad stuff win?

CHAPTER NINE

SAPPHIE stacked the last items into the dishwasher and then set about making caramel milkshakes—milk, lashings of caramel topping, and lots and lots of ice cream. She did her best to stop her gaze from drifting across to Liam. He sat hunched at the kitchen table. As he had done since she'd removed his dinner plate nearly half an hour ago.

Usually about now they made their excuses and retired to their separate rooms. She risked another glance at him. He'd been quiet during dinner—no doubt due to her sobering revelation earlier. Part of her couldn't believe she'd told him about her rape. It wasn't something she generally advertised. But his eyes had been so warm, and it had been so easy, almost natural to confide in him.

She still couldn't believe that kiss either—that heavenly, shake-her-to-her-foundations and freeze-her-in-her-shoes kiss.

Don't think about the kiss.

He started when she plonked a milkshake down in front of him. One corner of his mouth kicked up. 'Are you addicted to these things?'

'Hey, it's important for women to get plenty of calcium.'

'That's a yes, huh?'

'Ooh, you bet.'

She hunkered down in the chair opposite. They clinked glasses and drank. Sapphie licked away a milk moustache, noticed the way Liam watched that action and suddenly remembered why it was such a good idea to retire to her own room directly after dinner.

She cleared her throat. 'Tell me about Lucas.'

He stiffened. 'What?'

She bit back a sigh. 'He's Harry's father. I know I'm never going to get the opportunity to really know him, but I'd love to form a picture of who he was.'

He shifted on his chair, rolled his shoulders. 'What do you want to know?'

She wanted to hear whatever he wanted to tell her. She pointed to her milkshake. 'Did *he* have any addictions?'

He grinned then. She wasn't expecting it, and it stole her breath clean away. 'How long have you got?'

When he grinned like that, he could have all night if he wanted. 'I take it he was one of those kids who was into fads, huh?'

'When he was nine it was yo-yos—you should've seen his collection. By eleven it was model airplanes. At fifteen he was into retro heavy rock in a big way—drove us all mad with his electric guitar. I'm afraid on that score he had more enthusiasm than talent.'

She leant forward. 'He sounds so full of life!'

Liam sobered. 'He was.'

Mentally, she kicked herself. 'What made him happiest?'

'Riding, rodeos, and Mum's apple pie.'

That made her laugh. 'Was he a better rider then the rest of you?'

A low, sexy grin stretched all the way across his face. Her pulse skittered and jigged and hopped.

'As much as I hate to admit it—yes! You should've seen the cabinet full of his trophies for camp drafting and bronc riding.'

Her pulse refused to slow, and the memory of their kiss broke the surface of her consciousness again—that magical, heavenly kiss. She tried to pull back, tried not to notice how…masculine he looked in his polo shirt and jeans, or how the intriguing glimpse of hair that curled in the vee of his shirt seemed almost to beckon her. Her earlier lack of control had scared her rigid. There was no way she was ready for where a kiss like theirs could lead.

She'd never be ready.

Or would she?

The thought filtered into her mind. Ludicrous! She pushed it straight out again. She forced her attention back to Liam. His smile had gone.

'Mum packed them all away after…afterwards.'

'Perhaps you should drag some of them back out? For Harry?'

Very slowly, he nodded. 'Perhaps you're right.'

She could tell how proud he was of his little brother. And it was as if her questions had burst a dam open inside him, because without any further prompting from her he started talking about Lucas's rodeo victories, the scrapes he'd got into as a kid, and the old classic car he'd been trying to restore. His words gave life to the young man in the photographs— and Sapphie liked the picture they created.

'Did he ever speak about Emmy?' she asked when he finally fell silent.

He shook his head. 'Before he had his accident, though, I'd suspected he'd met someone.'

'How could you tell?'

'How do you tell those things about anyone who's close to you? He was distracted. He'd stare off into the distance with a goofy look on his face and then go all red when I teased him about it. And I knew he was planning another trip to Perth. It was unusual for him to make two trips in such quick succession.'

Across the table, his eyes met hers. 'I don't think Lucas meant to abandon your sister, Sapphie. I think he had the accident before he could get back to her.'

She stared down into her glass. 'I think that will mean a lot to her.'

'After his accident... Perhaps he didn't think Emmy would have wanted him. Being crippled, he wouldn't have thought he had anything to offer her.'

Sapphie swallowed back a lump. Poor Lucas. And poor Emmy.

'Liam, what happened to Lucas... it was tragic and awful. But you—your mum and dad, your brother and sister—you did everything you could to help him, to make things easier for him. It's unfair to expect more of yourselves. What Lucas did was his choice, his decision. It wasn't your fault.'

Liam didn't say anything, but his eyes burned into hers.

She reached across the table and touched his hand. 'Oh, but he sounds like such fun! No wonder Emmy fell for him. And no wonder you miss him so much.'

With that she got up and left the room before she did something really stupid—like walk around the table to kiss him. They'd both agreed that could never happen again.

For some reason, though, she couldn't get the thought of it out of her head.

'I can tell you're dying for a canter.'

It wasn't a question but a statement. Sapphie glanced at Liam and shrugged as they rode back into the yard. 'I'm perfectly happy.' With Harry on board neither one of them broke into anything faster than a trot.

The past four days had slid by with halcyon ease, and Sapphie swore there must be magic in the air at Newarra because there were so many joyful things to give thanks for.

For a start there was the way Harry no longer screamed when he woke from a nap and she wasn't there. He'd happily gabble away to his toys until she collected him from his cot. Then there was the way he'd started to crawl about the kitchen, the living room, the garden—in fact anywhere they put him down—with a newfound boldness and confidence that gladdened her heart.

Good things. Joyful things. Happy things.

Like the way the lines on Liam's face had started to fade, and the ease with which he could throw his head back now and laugh. The love that shone in his eyes whenever they rested on Harry.

The desire in them when they rested on her.

No, no…not desire! Gratitude, perhaps, and friendliness. That was what it was—friendliness. They were spending a lot of time together at the moment, that was all.

Most afternoons they took Jasper and Miss Lil out to explore the inner boundary of the property. What at first looked like an unending plain of red rock and spiky native grasses hid billabongs and native flowers, caves and fossils— places of wild beauty. The waterhole—a ten-minute ride upstream from where they'd first paddled with Harry—had made her gasp with longing.

A deep pool carved out of rock and filled with crystal-pure water, it was a tranquil, secret place. A waterfall trickled down from the rocks above. She'd wanted to dive in to test the clear coolness, to become a part of it. She'd wished they'd brought swimming costumes. But when she'd glanced across at the firm leanness that was Liam she'd thought maybe it was best that they hadn't.

Because, although she didn't want to admit it, heat flared between them at odd moments. A heat neither one of them was prepared to do anything about. A heat that had her tossing and turning at night. And, as she and Liam retired almost as soon as they'd finished dinner, there was a lot of night to toss and turn in.

'Rob!'

At Liam's shout, she blinked herself back into the present.

Rob appeared, and Liam handed Harry down to him. Sapphie held her breath. Rob had been at great pains to make friends with Harry in the last few days. He'd confided to Sapphie that he had six younger siblings and, although he hadn't said anything, she could tell he missed them. Harry didn't cry. He smiled.

He *smiled*!

'C'mon,' Liam said.

With a grin, he wheeled Jasper around and set off at a canter. Sapphie cast one glance at Harry—a happy Harry— and then with a cry of jubilation set off after Liam.

Her blood pumped and her spirits soared. The fact Harry felt secure enough to make friends with Rob had her heart expanding, giving her all the excuse she needed to throw herself fully into the wild exhilaration of a canter.

'Oh, that was wonderful!' she said, when they finally pulled their horses to a halt in the yard again. She beamed at Liam, and then at Harry and Rob. 'It's like flying!'

Harry waved his arms and gave a big baby laugh. She laughed too as she dismounted. 'Ooh, wouldn't you love to try that, mister? Well, I'm afraid you're going to have to wait until you're older.'

'When he's older,' Rob said, handing him over to take Miss Lil's reins, 'he'll put us all to shame. I'll take care of the horses, boss,' he added, moving to take Jasper's reins too.

'Thanks, Rob.' Liam swung to Sapphie. 'Here, I'll take Harry. He's starting to get heavy.'

She handed him over without a murmur or a pang. She enjoyed seeing them together too much now for that. Her blood danced in her veins as they strolled back to the house. She could barely contain herself to a walk. She wanted to dance and skip. 'Ooh, I loved that!'

Liam's grin reached all the way down to curl her toes. 'I kind of noticed.'

'You know, I think I'm going to have to get a little piece of land on the outskirts of Perth somewhere, with a little cottage, and a horse and chickens, and…' Her words petered out.

She didn't want to think about her life away from here just yet. A life without Harry. When she glanced across, though, it was Liam her eyes rested on first. 'Perhaps when I win the Lottery,' she gulped.

Liam stared straight out to the front, his lips an uncompromising line. 'Perhaps you'll just have to visit Newarra and Jarndirri more often.'

She'd have smiled, because his words sounded more like an order than a suggestion, but it suddenly hit her that she had to leave Newarra—and soon. She'd let herself forget that over the last few days. 'Perhaps that's the answer,' she managed.

She guessed her words hadn't emerged as cheerily as she'd meant them to, because his gaze speared her, the laser-like blue of his eyes trying to plumb her soul. She turned away before he could see too much, and discovered they'd mounted the veranda's back steps without her realising it.

'I'll go clean Harry up and put him down for his nap, and then it's caramel milkshakes in the usual spot if you're up for it.' She took Harry. 'Unless there's paperwork you need to get done?' A time out from each other might be a good thing.

Liam eased back, thumbs hooked in the belt loops of his jeans. 'There's nothing that can't wait.' One corner of his mouth kicked up. 'Caramel milkshakes sound…perfect.'

While he spoke, his blue eyes travelled over her in slow appraisal. It made her instantly aware of how she'd defiantly tossed her oversized shirt back into her suitcase today. Perhaps that had been premature? Provocative?

But she knew the shirt wouldn't have made a difference— not to the way she felt and not to the way Liam treated her.

'That canter has put some colour in your cheeks.' He pushed the door open for her with a kind of lazy, knowing grace. 'I'll let you see to Harry, then, shall I?'

He grinned—one of those slow, sexy numbers he'd grown so adept at lately—as if he knew the effect he was having on her. She kicked herself into action. 'Uh, right.' And then fled.

She dawdled over changing Harry's nappy, in cleaning his hands and face, and in singing to him as he settled down to his nap. Not only because she needed the time to gather her scattered wits, but because she meant to treasure every last one of her moments with him.

They'd have to last her a long time once she returned to Perth.

When his breathing grew slow and rhythmic, she finally turned away. She paused in her bedroom doorway, straightened her shirt and mentally girded her loins. 'Caramel milkshakes,' she murmured. 'Easy-peasy.'

She'd keep it light and fun. *No heat.*

She blew out a breath. *No sweat.*

She strode along the corridor—chin up, shoulders back. She closed her eyes and dragged in a breath. She opened them and—

Oh! She skidded to a halt, coming within millimetres of slamming smack-bang into Liam's *near-naked* body as he emerged from the bathroom. And she had no hope of fighting back the heat that spiralled through her. No hope at all.

He wore a towel—nothing else. It covered the essentials, but only just, because it rode so low on his hips that, with an oath, he had to grab at it and haul it up.

Fresh from the shower, his hair gleamed darker, curling at his neck and behind his ears. She watched a stray droplet of water trickle down the strong column of his throat to his collarbone and her mouth went dry.

Dark hair curled across his chest and her fingers itched to reach out and touch. That sculpted chest, the muscles in those shoulders and arms, were the result of hard physical labour. That deep golden tan told her that some mornings Liam did that hard physical labour minus his shirt.

Her limbs went languid. Her eyes followed the spattering of hair trailing down his stomach to disappear beneath the line of the towel—a flat stomach, lean hips...powerful thighs. She couldn't have summoned up a more outstanding example of masculine perfection if she'd tried. She had to grip her hands in front of her to stop from reaching out and touching. She knew what he'd feel like—firm and silken. And hot.

'Sapphie?'

'Hmm…?' She couldn't drag her gaze away.

'Sapphie!'

The sharp tone made her blink, forced her to drag her gaze up to his face. That wasn't any hardship. His face was as beautiful as the rest of him. Lean and hard, but beautiful.

He swept his hand over his hair. 'If you don't stop looking at me like that—'

She stared at his fingers, imagined them trailing a path over her body—discovering, teasing…pleasing. Her breath caught. It would be magic to—

'Sapphie!'

She forced herself to focus on his face again. She stared at him dumbly.

Yikes! *What she was doing!* She stepped back so fast she whacked the back of her head on the wall behind. She didn't even wince. She turned and fled to the kitchen.

Oh! She pressed her hands to her cheeks. She pulled them away to wring them. She turned in a circle. Caramel milkshakes—that was what she should be doing, making. She stared about the kitchen, but she couldn't seem to fix her eyes on a single item. She gave up and sped out through the living room's French doors to collapse on the bench outside. She drew her knees up to her chest and rested her forehead on them, concentrated on slowing her breathing.

'You want to talk about that?'

Sapphie practically jumped out of her skin. Her feet hit the boards with a thud as she spun on the bench.

Liam stood in the doorway—not nearly naked, thank heavens. He wore denim jeans and a polo shirt. His feet were bare, which would explain why she hadn't heard him. Though she had a feeling that if Liam didn't want to be heard he wouldn't be heard, regardless of what he wore on his feet.

'No, of course I don't want to talk about that!' She found herself on her feet, shaking. She forced herself to sit again. She couldn't meet his eyes. 'Why would I want to talk about what a fool I just made of myself?'

She dragged both hands through her hair. 'Heck, Liam, if you'd ogled *me* like that I'd have had your hide.'

But she'd never known she could desire a man again, let alone crave one the way she craved Liam. She couldn't act upon it…oh, no, *no*. But she didn't know how on earth she was supposed to deal with it. Or how to hide the effect he had on her.

Liam settled on the other end of the bench from her. Embarrassment surged through her so thick she could barely stand to glance at him.

'Sapphie, what you're feeling, experiencing…it's normal, you know?'

'Normal?' She pushed the word out between gritted teeth. 'That wasn't normal. A…a teenage girl—a teenage *boy*!—would've shown more finesse, more manners, than I just did.' She turned. '*You* don't feel it. Not like that!'

'Don't feel it?' He gaped at her. 'The way you were looking at me made me so hot I thought the skin would blister from my body!'

Her jaw dropped. 'I…' She dragged it back up, realising his admission didn't help.

'Your body has needs. Needs you've denied for the last seven years. They've flared up now, for whatever reason, and it's taken you off guard. So, yes, Sapphie, what you're feeling *is* normal.'

'I don't want normal,' she wailed. 'I want to go back to how it was before.'

'Maybe it's a sign.'

'Of what?'

'That it's time for you to move on, start dating again.'

She stared at him in horror. 'Oh, no, no, no.' She shook her head. Once. Twice. Hard. But it suddenly hit her—when once

finding herself alone with a near-naked man would have in-
duced terror, seeing Liam in nothing but a towel...

No terror. Not even the faintest tingling of alarm. Self-pres-
ervation hadn't even come into the equation.

'Sapphie, you're young, you're lovely. You deserve to find
the man of your dreams.'

'There's no such thing. He doesn't exist.' Her voice wobbled,
though, revealing her sudden lack of certainty. 'Besides, I *have*
dated.' She'd chosen safety in numbers—gone out in a group a
few times, a couple of times even double-dated. She'd never let
anything happen between her and any of the guys she'd dated,
though. She'd made sure she'd never been left alone with them.

Liam leant towards her, his eyes warm and his smile kind,
as if he knew exactly the kind of dates she'd been on. 'Any
man worth his salt would take his time, Sapphie. He wouldn't
rush you. He'd go slow.'

It was as if he'd tapped into all her fears and could see each
and every one of them. Would Liam take his time? The
thought made her slow burn.

'What that man did to you, Sapphie, it was a terrible thing.
I'm not trying to downplay it, but don't define your life based
on that one experience. Don't let the badness win.'

Start dating again? Her throat went tight. All her limbs
went languid. 'That's fine talk coming from you, Mr I'm-
never-going-to-marry-again.' The criticism implicit in her
words was lost through her sheer breathlessness, though.

He grinned. 'I'm older than you, remember? I've already
had my fair share of dates.'

'Right,' she muttered.

He reached out and took her hand. Her tongue plastered
itself to the roof of her mouth.

'All I'm saying is that I think you should mull it over, not
dismiss it out of hand.'

She couldn't unglue her tongue—not while he held her
hand—so she just shrugged and nodded.

'Good.' He released her hand and rose. 'I better take a rain-check on that milkshake. There's a few things I need to sort out with my overseer.'

She kept her gaze stoically to the front, and didn't watch him as he strode along the veranda and down the steps. Start dating again? She swallowed. A week ago that would have been out of the question. Her pulse started to race. But now…

CHAPTER TEN

LIAM stared at the calendar on his desk. He abandoned the accounts to seize it. Three days! There were only three days left of his and Sapphie's agreement. That couldn't be right, surely? She'd only just arrived.

He counted back. Sapphie had been at Newarra for almost two whole weeks. Such a short time, but…but a part of him felt as if it had known her for ever.

He pushed that thought away. It implied a level of intimacy he had no intention of exploring.

He replaced the calendar. Three days left, and he had no idea yet what she thought would be best for Harry.

A solid weight settled in the middle of his chest. He could provide a good home for Harry. She had to see that. *She had to.*

The thought of being separated from Harry now… Bile rose in his throat. He loved his nephew with a fierceness that shocked him. The same way Sapphie loved Harry, he acknowledged.

He pressed his fingers to his eyes and deliberately recalled each and every one of the charges she'd levelled at him when he'd revealed that he wanted to adopt Harry. He drummed his fingers. He'd changed. He'd prove it to her. They'd… They'd go on a picnic. He glanced at his watch—right now!

He'd show her how much fun he could be, how easygoing. He'd show her what a wonderful home he could give Harry.

He made rolls out of towels and swimsuits. Sapphie was shorter than Lacey, and a little smaller, but he figured one of Lacey's old swimming costumes would fit her just fine. He grabbed saddlebags and made for the kitchen.

Sapphie glanced up from making the men's lunches. 'Finished already?'

He'd told her he was doing the accounts rather than mending cattleyards today. Mustering would start in earnest soon, and he wanted everything else under control before then.

Harry was far more important than the accounts, though.

Harry crawled across to Liam. Gripping handfuls of denim, he pulled himself up to a standing position and stood there, balanced against Liam's leg, grinning proudly. Liam's heart practically fell out of his chest.

'Hey, Tiger!' He picked him up and tossed him in the air until Harry chortled with glee. It was Sapphie's grin that speared into his gut, though.

'I'm over the accounts,' he muttered, suddenly self-conscious. 'I thought we might skive off and have a picnic. What do you think?'

'I...' He wasn't sure if she was searching for a reason to say yes, or a reason to say no. Her eyes rested on Harry and her whole face softened. It stayed soft when she glanced back at Liam. 'I think that's a lovely idea.'

He let out the breath he'd been holding. 'Great. I'm starving, and something smells good in here!' He felt as awkward as a teenager on a first date.

He shuffled back a pace, rolled his shoulders. This wasn't a date.

Sapphie set a basket on the table, covered it with a cloth. 'That's the men's lunches made. Just give me ten minutes to put our lunch together and grab a couple of things for Harry, and then we'll be set to go.'

'No rush.' She wore stretch denim jeans that fitted her to perfection, and a faded blue T-shirt that somehow picked out the blonde highlights in her hair. Liam's skin went tight. Some time in the last few days she'd stopped wearing those baggy sweaters and over-sized shirts.

'Uh, Harry and I'll wait outside—get out from under your feet.'

She raised an eyebrow, but he didn't hang around to explain. He pushed out through the back door and tried to chase her scent out of his lungs with the clean, dry air. Sapphie, scented with her morning's baking, smelt good enough to eat.

And he'd just discovered he was a very hungry man.

'Gluttony is a deadly sin,' he said to Harry, lowering his frame to the top step and jiggling his nephew on his knee.

'I can make you a sandwich now if you want,' Sapphie said from directly behind him.

He turned to find her standing at the screen door, partially obscured by its wire mesh. Her scent wafted out to him. 'No, thanks, I'm fine.'

'But you just said—'

'I can wait till lunch.' He worked on keeping his voice steady. 'Something smells great, that's all. What have you been baking?'

'Nothing. I baked yesterday.'

He turned further around on the step. 'Then what smells so good?' The air smelt of vanilla, and a hint of nutmeg, and…caramel sauce?

'Might be something I cut up for the lunches, or…' She shrugged. 'Search me.'

No, not a good idea. Definitely not a good idea.

'Did you want a drink while you wait?'

'Nah.' He wanted to rid his senses of that scent, that was what he wanted to do. Then he remembered his manners. 'Thank you for asking, though. Harry and me, we're just fine—aren't we, Harry?'

She disappeared. He wiped his forearm across his brow. He didn't need a drink. He needed a cold shower.

He was ready for her when she came out with the saddlebags. He took them from her immediately. She glanced at the towel rolls he had tossed over one shoulder, and at Harry balanced on his hip. 'What can I take?'

'Nothing. It's all good.'

'But you're carrying everything.'

'So?'

He couldn't help it. He wanted to make things easy for her, protect her. After everything she'd been through she deserved that much.

She disappeared back inside the house and emerged a moment later carrying the basket that held the men's lunches. He opened his mouth to tell her not to worry, that someone would be along to collect it, but before he could she said, 'Let me feel useful. It'll save someone the trip across.'

If he'd had a free arm he'd have slung it across her shoulders. On reflection, it was probably just as well he didn't.

Sapphie's grin when they wound down through the shallow gully to emerge at the waterhole half an hour later told him this picnic was a good idea. A very good idea. Even if he *had* spent most of the last thirty minutes doing his level best not to stare at her and that very good seat of hers.

Stare? Don't you mean ogle?

He swallowed. His hand clenched about the reins. He had no intention of laying so much as a finger on the generous and delectable Sapphie. He might not be able to take a cold shower, but there was an entire waterhole full of cold water at his disposal.

'Swim first, lunch later.'

'But I don't have a swimsuit,' Sapphie wailed.

He pointed to the towel roll attached to the back of her saddle. 'One of Lacey's old swimsuits is in there.'

She dismounted and retrieved the towel roll. She'd have unhitched the saddlebags too, but Liam said, 'I'll take care of those.'

He handed Harry down to her, and it suddenly hit him that Sapphie was used to doing everything for herself—not just most things, but everything. The thought slid in under his skin and niggled at him.

'What's wrong?'

He glanced down to find her holding Harry close. He cleared his face immediately. 'Sorry, just remembered something about the accounts.'

'Bad?'

'Nothing I can't sort.'

Liar! He couldn't help Sapphie, or give her what she needed—not in any real way. It was she who'd helped him. It didn't stop him from wanting to look after her.

With a superhuman effort, he kept his face scowl-free. 'I'm going to unsaddle the horses and tether them over here. Why don't you set us up on the strip of sand over there?'

With a shrug, she ambled off. Liam watched the rhythmic sway of her hips until a flock of northern rosellas dipped through the gully, their blue and black feathers flashing against the landscape. With a smothered oath he leapt off Jasper and led both horses to a grassy spot, and gave himself a serious talking-to before rejoining Sapphie and Harry.

He found them sitting on a beach towel, Sapphie surveying the swimsuit he'd given her. 'It is okay, isn't it?' he said, suddenly unsure.

'It's pink!'

His lips twitched. 'Lacey's a girly-girl.'

'A girly-girl? Growing up out here?'

He lowered himself down to the towel beside her. Her scent hit him again. 'Lacey is a first-class cattle breeder. She's capable and independent. But she's a girly-girl. She likes jewellery and trinkets and baubles—things that twinkle and glitter. She likes clothes with lace and frills and tassels. And her favourite colour is pink.'

It occurred to him that he'd never seen Sapphie wear pink.

With an effort of will, he kept a straight face. 'I didn't think you'd care about the colour.'

Her chin shot up. 'Of course I don't! That'd be silly. Especially way out here in the Never-Never. But…'

'But?'

'It's a bikini! I *never* wear bikinis.'

He blinked. He hadn't given *that* a second thought. He'd just grabbed the first of Lacey's swimsuits that had come to hand. 'Why not? Sapphie, you sure don't need to be self-conscious. You have a great figure, and you'd look fabulous in—'

He broke off, suddenly remembering what had happened to her, and he knew he couldn't even begin to understand what that attack had done to her. He dragged a hand down his face and recalled those baggy sweaters. He might not know how it felt, but he could do his best to make her feel safe now.

He pulled his hand from his face to take the swimsuit from her. He surveyed the top, and then the bottoms. 'You know, most women's basketball teams wear something similar to this.'

She opened her mouth, then closed it again to stare at the two strips of fabric he held.

'This isn't one of those skimpy numbers,' he continued. 'This is a crop top. And these…' He held up the bottoms and tried not to imagine Sapphie's neat little behind filling them out. 'If these were black nylon instead of pink Lycra they'd be the same as those pants Lacey used to wear for gymnastics at boarding school.'

Sapphie smiled at that. 'I had to wear those too.'

'And, apart from all that, Harry and I don't count.'

She eased back to stare at him. 'What on earth are you talking about?'

'As an audience—me and Harry don't count. Harry is your nephew, and he's not going to care what kind of swimsuit you wear. And I'm Harry's uncle, which practically makes you and me family. Where swimsuits are concerned, family don't count.'

Her eyes narrowed, and he wondered if she'd seen the

flaw of that particular argument, so he rushed on with, 'But if you really don't want to wear it then perhaps you could put my T-shirt on over the top.' He flicked the sleeve. 'Once this old thing is wet it'll practically hang down to your knees.'

She opened her mouth, but he leant across and pressed a finger to her lips. 'Sapphie, do whatever makes you feel most comfortable. Harry and me, we don't care what you wear—the decision is up to you. Now, I'm going to go and get into my board shorts behind those bushes over there.' He leapt up and made for said bushes. 'No peeking.'

'I'd do no such thing!'

She swung away with a gasp, and he figured she'd just remembered the way she'd stared at him when he'd emerged from his shower that day. The memory made him grin.

Her cheeks were pink when he returned, but he made no comment. He dropped his shirt beside her, picked up Harry, and made for the cool clear water.

He and Harry both gasped as the water closed over them. They splashed and laughed and swam, and Liam did his best not to notice what Sapphie did on shore—though he clocked the exact moment she rose and headed towards the bushes to change.

He deliberately turned his back. The temptation to catch even the tiniest glimpse of her naked was too great a temptation to toy with.

Harry loved the water, and he provided an entertaining distraction, but Liam could pick out the sounds as Sapphie moved back towards them—the shaking out of a towel, the pebbles shifting beneath her feet as she made her way down to the water. He told himself he would only turn around if she gave him a sign.

'How's the water?'

He turned around. She wore his shirt. He tried to hide his disappointment. 'The water is great.'

Her eyes widened when her feet first touched the water.

'See, I told you,' he called out. His shirt came to the tops of her thighs. She looked cute, coltish…sweet. 'Dare you to dive right in.'

And she did. Just like that. She emerged not too far from him and directed a jet of water straight at him. Harry chortled as if it was the funniest thing he'd ever seen. Liam splashed her back. Harry chortled more and splashed everyone.

Liam couldn't remember the last time he'd had so much fun. The three of them dived and frolicked and laughed. Harry's laughter, Sapphie's laughter, loosened something inside him, making it easier and easier for him to laugh too.

At one point Sapphie eased back. 'You know, it's actually hideously uncomfortable swimming in your T-shirt, Liam. No offence.'

'None taken.'

His tongue cleaved to the roof of his mouth when she stood up in waist-high water, peeled his shirt off over her head and spread it out on a nearby rock to dry. She wore the pink bikini beneath it and she was…beautiful!

With a grin she dived under the water, as if to test her newfound sense of freedom. She surfaced right beside him. 'Thank you for lending me your shirt,' she whispered. 'It helped me get used to the idea of this.' She touched the shoulder strap of the bikini top.

'Any time,' he managed. He reached out, touched the backs of his fingers to her cheek. 'I just want you to feel safe here, Sapphie.'

'I know. And I do. Thank you.'

Her eyes darkened and he snatched his hand back. 'Right! Time to teach Harry to swim.'

Sapphie called a halt to the fun and games a little while later. 'Enough!' She laughed. 'It has to be time for lunch. I'm famished.'

So was he.

He followed her out of the water and tried to disguise his

pang when she pulled on her T-shirt and planted her hat on her head. She dried Harry off, then pulled his little shirt and tiny shorts on too.

'I know we have a shady spot here.' She glanced at the rocks to their left, whose overhang protected them from the sun. 'But it's never wise to underestimate the sun at this time of the day. Harry and I aren't used to it being so warm at this time of the year yet.' She glanced across at his shirt, drying on a rock. 'I'm sorry about—'

'It's practically dry.' He dragged it on over his head. He wanted her to feel safe.

Being clothed was safer for both of them. Though he couldn't help noticing her T-shirt dropped only an inch or so below her waist, leaving the honeyed flesh of her glorious legs exposed. Lovely legs that—

He dragged his gaze away. Ogling her was not a method designed to make her feel safe.

Harry grabbed his bottle the moment Sapphie produced it, curled up on the towel between them, and with a contented sigh closed his eyes.

Sapphie leant across and brushed the baby curls back from his face. 'He's had so much fun.' She glanced up at Liam, her smile warm, as if he were the sole reason for Harry's fun. 'I have too.'

It would be so easy to lean across and kiss her now.

He edged back. 'That makes three of us.'

She touched a hand to her face. She frowned, then swallowed. 'It's going to be a little awkward trying to eat around Harry like this. Do you think you could move him more into the shade just there?'

Liam did, and Sapphie unpacked sandwiches and fruit, thick slices of cake and a Thermos of tea. They ate in silence—not a fraught silence, but a companionable, contented quiet.

At least it wasn't fraught as long as he didn't glance across at her and her lovely and far too tempting curves. He concentrated on staring out at the landscape—at the sandstone and granite rocks that enclosed the waterhole and rose at its far end to a sheer cliff, where the waterfall descended in a long, easy flow. The contrasting red and grey of the rocks, the washed-out white-gold of nearby tussocks of grass and the clear deep blue of the sky above. Its peace and grandeur stole into his soul. Combined with the scent of the woman beside him, it turned this place into paradise.

With a contented sigh, he eased down until he lay on his back. 'They were great sandwiches, Sapphie. And great tea and cake.'

'Ooh, and a great idea,' she returned, settling back on her towel too. The tiniest of sighs escaped her. 'This place is heavenly.'

'Yep.'

They were quiet for a bit, listening to the breeze ruffle the grass and the rhythmic splash of the waterfall, the occasional cry of a bird.

He turned to glance at her profile. 'Sapphie?'

'Hmm?'

She didn't turn to meet his gaze. Her lips were far too full and tempting in profile. He wanted to taste them. He dragged his head back round until he was staring heavenwards again.

Her lips are off-limits.

He ground his eyes shut for a moment. 'Do you know there's only three days left on our agreement?'

'Uh-huh.'

He couldn't tell anything from her tone. He cursed himself for starting this conversation while they were flat on their backs and staring up at the sky. He wanted to see her face. He wanted to know what she was thinking.

There was only one way to know that for sure...

He pulled in a breath. 'I need to know what you're thinking. Where Harry's concerned, that is.' He swallowed.

His mouth had gone strangely dry. 'Are you for me or against me?'

She didn't say anything for a long moment, then, 'You remember the night before last, when you put Harry to bed on your own?'

He'd asked if he could. He'd wanted to know if Harry would settle for him. He'd wanted to sing Lucas's song to him again.

'I didn't stay in the kitchen. I crept down the hallway and stood outside the bedroom door to listen.'

He frowned at the sky. 'Why?' He'd thought she trusted him.

'Curiosity, I guess. And…and I was feeling a bit left out.'

He found her hand and squeezed it. 'You should've joined us.'

'No, it's right that you and Harry should have your own time together.' She paused. 'You talked to him about Lucas.'

He dropped her hand. He wanted to get up and walk away. He wanted to stay where he was. He didn't know *what* he wanted to do.

She slipped her hand back inside his and squeezed. He let out the breath he held. 'Harry is going to want to know all about his dad when he's growing up. I thought I'd try it out and see if I could do it, talk about Lucas.'

'I thought you did a wonderful job.'

Her words warmed him. 'Ever since the night you and I talked about him I—'

Her hand tightened in his. 'You what?'

He glared at the sky. 'Do you know how angry I am with him for giving up? For not fighting on a little bit longer?'

'Oh, Liam.'

'I blamed myself for his death because it was easier than coming to terms with the truth—that he left us! He made the decision to leave us.'

He was suddenly glad they were lying on their backs and staring up at the sky. Beside him he could sense Sapphie fighting her desire to sit up. He squeezed her hand, silently asking her to stay where she was. At the moment, if she offered him any physical comfort he'd take it—all of it. And they'd both regret it afterwards.

After a moment she squeezed his hand back and remained where she was. 'He must've been in a lot of pain, a lot of…despair.'

'I know that too.'

He sensed she'd turned her head to look at him. 'Are you still angry with him?'

'A little,' he admitted. But it had grown less and less the more he talked about Lucas. His lips twisted. 'I had an epiphany the other night. You want to hear about it?'

'Sure.'

'I suddenly realised I was never going to stop missing him. Startling revelation, huh?'

She didn't laugh, even though he'd deliberately made fun of himself. 'You don't realise that stuff until you lose someone close to you,' she murmured.

He thought about her mother, her sister. It occurred to him that he'd always known she'd understand. 'I also realised I could make the decision to miss him in a good way, or miss him in a bad way.' He turned his head to meet her gaze. 'I've decided to miss him in a good way. For Harry's sake. And my own.'

Her smile was as dazzling as sheet lightning that could illuminate an entire plain in the darkness of a storm. 'I'm glad.'

'I want to be as good a father as I can to Harry. I need to know if you think I can do that.'

She pursed her lips and surveyed him. His heart started to pound. He didn't know if she was teasing him or not.

'You want to know something? These days it doesn't actually look as if it hurts you to smile. And you know what else? I believe I even heard you laugh earlier today.'

She *was* teasing him!

A grin grew inside him. 'Yeah, well, I'm finding babies can have that kind of effect on a person.' But it was more than that. When Sapphie was around she made it easy to laugh.

He and Harry would still laugh when she left, but they'd miss her.

She'd come back for visits.

Or…she could stay longer, couldn't she?

If he asked her to.

A frown built up inside him. He shook it off to focus back on their conversation. 'Does that mean you're going to advise Emmy…?'

'That you're the right person to adopt Harry?' Their eyes met and held. 'Yes, it does.'

Unaccountably, his eyes prickled and burned. He had to haul in a breath and hold it for a moment before he could trust himself to speak. 'Thank you.'

'You don't need to thank me.'

Yes, he did.

'And, Liam?'

'Yes?'

'You're killing my hand.'

He relaxed his grip immediately, grimacing an apology.

Her eyes hadn't left his. 'You do know the final decision doesn't rest with me, but with Emmy?'

'Yes.'

Her gaze abruptly turned skyward. 'There are some things I need to tell you.'

His stomach clenched. So far she'd avoided talking about Emmy and her reasons for giving Harry up. Was she finally ready to trust him with the truth?

'Can we have this conversation sitting up?'

He sat up immediately. She followed more slowly. She freed her hand from his and her gaze slid away to the waterfall. He had a feeling, though, that she didn't really see it.

'Emmy has made a lot of mistakes in the last few years.'

She turned, her eyes filled with pleading. 'But I truly believe she wants to make amends for all that.' She glanced back at the sleeping child.

'Starting with Harry?' he asked softly.

'Yes.' She moistened her lips. 'I wanted you to get to know Harry without other things intruding. And I wanted to protect Emmy for as long as I could too. But I see now that Emmy doesn't need protecting from you, Liam.'

His heart started to expand.

'A few weeks ago Emmy was arrested on drug charges. It's not her first offence.'

A shadow of weariness passed over her face. Liam reached out and pushed a strand of hair back behind her ear. He wanted to spare her having to go into details when they so obviously distressed her. 'Sapphie, I'm sorry.'

'She knows jail is no place for a baby. She wants Harry to have a new start in life.' She paused. 'And maybe…maybe eventually she'll find a way to rebuild her own life.'

'I'll offer her any support I can,' he promised.

'Thank you,' she whispered.

'I'll have to go and see her.'

She nodded. 'I know.'

'If it does work out—if Emmy agrees that I can adopt Harry—will you stay on for another fortnight? Till Beattie gets back? To help Harry fully settle in at Newarra?'

Her eyes widened. 'I'd love to.'

She stared at him, her eyes round and her cute little mouth ajar, and he couldn't help it. He found himself leaning towards her…

He stopped short. He shouldn't kiss her. She'd been through too much. Kissing her wouldn't be fair. It would give her all the wrong ideas.

Or the right ones? A voice whispered through him.

'Liam?'

He swallowed. 'I…'

She glanced at his lips, and then into his eyes. She didn't hesitate—she leant forward and placed her lips on his.

Magic! The breath eased out of him. He couldn't move away, but he was careful not to move in closer, did what he could to avoid full body, skin-on-skin contact. But he couldn't resist tasting her just this once.

With excruciating slowness, thoroughness, he moved his lips over hers. He wanted to memorise their every line and curve and indentation. He nipped at her bottom lip gently, then ran his tongue over it back and forth, relishing her soft warmth and the sweet heat.

She gasped and he half expected her to draw back, but she didn't. She pressed her lips more firmly to his, moved them against his just as slowly as he had, and then with alarming seductiveness her tongue traced the line of his bottom lip. His insides turned to molten fire.

He pulled back, his breathing ragged. He deserved to get burned, playing with fire like that!

In one swift motion she was on her knees. She seized his face in her hands and kissed him—open-mouthed. She took him so much by surprise he fell back, and she fell too—sprawling on top of him. His hands went about her waist to steady her, his fingers sliding against her bare flesh. He didn't have any hope of hiding his arousal. He told himself to put her from him, but his fingers curved against her bare flesh, caressing it instead.

Her eyes widened. She moved against him experimentally. White-hot shafts of need shot through him. 'I didn't know it could be like this,' she whispered, her breath teasing his lips. 'So…right.'

He tried to open his mouth, tried to make words come out, but before he could her hand snaked up under his shirt to trace the contours of his chest, raking it lightly with her fingernails. 'I've wanted to do this ever since I saw you all but naked.'

Her artless confession had him gritting his teeth. When she

shifted against him again—restless and searching—he rolled her over. He couldn't think straight when she moved against him like that and—

She arched up into him and he groaned. 'Sapphie, you have no idea what you're doing.'

'I know precisely what I'm doing. I'm trying to seduce you.' Her hands explored his shoulders, his throat. He stared at the shine on her lips and tried to fight the need surging through him. She cocked an eyebrow, moved beneath him. 'How am I doing?'

He gulped. 'Brilliantly. Ten out of ten.'

She smiled—radiant.

'Sapphie, I—'

She pressed her fingers to his lips. 'I don't want to talk about promises or tomorrow, Liam. Can't I have this one moment in time to find out just how good it can be between a man and a woman? No promises, no tomorrows.'

She wanted him to make love to her? To have a chance to chase some of the shadows from her eyes…? He ached to make love to her—slowly, tenderly, thoroughly. He wanted to show her precisely how good it could be.

'Please, Liam.'

He couldn't resist her when she stared at him like that.

'I didn't know it could be this…good.'

He trailed a lazy path from armpit to hip, and back again. His hands were gentle, teasing… slow. Satisfaction gripped him when she shivered, when her glorious eyes turned a delicious smoky green.

'I'll let you into a little secret,' he murmured. 'Neither did I.'

He traced the outline of her bottom lip with his thumb, then tipped her head up for his kiss—warm, tender…*right*.

CHAPTER ELEVEN

SAPPHIE became Liam's lover. Or perhaps he became hers. She wasn't sure how one referred to these things. But for the next three days she and Liam made love.

He was so tender, so gentle…so generous. He'd made her feel safe. And then he'd made her feel cherished, beautiful and free.

He'd left for Perth yesterday afternoon, so he could meet with Emmy first thing today. He'd taken photographs with him of Lucas. He'd sworn to Sapphie that he'd break the news of Lucas's death gently. Not that he'd needed to swear that—she knew he would. She knew he'd treat her little sister with consideration and respect.

He'd promised to broach the subject of Harry's adoption gently too. He hadn't needed to promise that either. She'd given him a letter for Emmy—a letter telling her all about Newarra, telling her what a wonderful life Harry could have here. Telling her how much Liam loved Harry already. And vice versa.

She knew it was important that Liam make this trip. Harry's whole future depended on it. Yet it didn't stop the yearning from pulsing through her—the yearning to be in his arms, to be pressing her mouth to his skin, sliding her arms around his waist—to be touching and tasting him. The yearning for him to be here with her, so they could lose themselves in the glory of their lovemaking.

A sigh slipped out of her. Making love… She'd not been afraid. Not with Liam. Not once.

Because you love him.

Her knees promptly gave out, plonking her down to a kitchen chair. *Love him?*

Harry crawled over and pulled himself up to a standing position, leaning against her knees and patting them. 'Sapph, Sapph, Sapph.'

She picked him up and cuddled him. 'Hungry, beautiful boy?' He snuggled in against her, pulling her heart tight. 'It must be time for your afternoon nap, mister.'

In a daze, she fixed his bottle and settled him in his cot. She drifted back into the kitchen…made a pot of tea.

Love Liam?

Of course she loved Liam! How could she not? How could a woman resist a man who loved a baby as much as Liam loved Harry? How could she resist a man who was determined to do what was right—not just for Harry, but for her and Emmy too, not to mention his own family?

Liam was confident and capable—a leader—but he was kind too. The combination was lethal. 'I didn't stand a chance,' she murmured out loud. Not after she factored in those broad shoulders and lean hips, that sexy grin and his sheer generosity as a lover.

And to think she'd told him she didn't want to talk about promises! She did now. She wanted to promise him everything. Had she really said she'd just wanted those moments out of time? No, she wanted for ever. With Liam. She wanted to build a beautiful golden life with him and Harry and whoever else came along and—

She couldn't have it!

Pain scrunched her chest up so tight she had to hunch over and hug her stomach. Her face crumpled. She couldn't have that golden life. Liam had said he'd never marry again. And even if he changed his mind…

She started to shake. Once he found out her secret he'd shun her and send her away.

And Sapphie would deserve it. He'd hate her as much as she hated herself, and the realisation tortured her. Even if Liam changed his mind, nothing long-term could ever happen between them. Because of Harry—because she didn't deserve him—because she didn't deserve to play such a large role in his life. In fact it would probably be in Harry's best interests if she just disappeared from his life completely.

She didn't have the strength to do that.

She pressed the heels of her hands to her eyes. Lingering at Newarra like this, playing happy families, it was all a terrible, deceitful lie. If she stayed, she'd end up hurting the two people she loved the most.

She dragged her hands away. She'd do her best to be a good auntie to Harry. She knew what it was like to grow up without any extended family—she wanted something more for him, something better. But she could never be anything more to him than that.

She forced herself to straighten. She forced the tears back. She didn't deserve the relief they would bring. She didn't deserve a decent, honest man like Liam or an innocent like Harry. She'd known that for the last seven years. She'd known that when she'd brought Harry to Newarra. Dreams she'd never been able to fully extinguish had somehow taken seed here and started to blossom, and she'd been silly enough to let herself get swept up in them.

Stupid girl!

She stared at the kitchen clock—tried to make sense of the numbers, of big hands and little hands. Liam would be home soon, and she knew exactly what she had to do.

It was time to stop dreaming.

Liam couldn't temper the thrill that shot through him when his single-engine Cessna touched down in the gathering dusk at Newarra. In a few more minutes he could sweep Sapphie up in his arms, pull her in close and kiss her until he made her gasp and cling to his shoulders.

He loved the way his kisses made her eyes go smoky and her voice husky. He revelled in her growing confidence and boldness. He'd missed her in his bed last night, and he wanted to lose himself in her softness, her generosity, her...*passion* as soon as he could.

Passion, he'd started to realise, that had been lacking from his life for far too long.

Rob was waiting for him when he jumped down from the light plane. 'Hey, boss, thought you might like a lift back to the homestead.'

The airplane hangar was two kilometres from the homestead. In his current mood, Liam felt as if he could sprint them easily enough. One corner of his mouth kicked up. It would be better to conserve his energy for more enjoyable things. 'Thanks, Rob.'

'Good trip?'

'Not bad.'

When they reached the homestead they both nodded and muttered, 'Night.' Men of few words. A trip to the city always reminded him why he felt he belonged out here.

His anticipation ratcheted up a notch as he moved towards the house. He pushed open the back door. And...

And...nothing.

Sapphie didn't race over to him, even though she was in the kitchen stirring something that was bubbling away on the stove and smelt pretty darn good. Normally she'd drop her spoon and rush over to wind her arms around his neck, with a wicked gleam in her eye that would evoke an instant response in him without fail.

He moved towards her, intent on pulling her back against him to press kisses to the nape of her neck and run his hands over her curves until she moaned, but the smile she turned on him stopped him dead.

'Hey, Liam, you're back. How was your trip?'

There was something wrong with that smile. 'The trip was fine.'

'Sit down. Tea or a beer?'

'Beer.' He pulled out a chair and tried to work out what was wrong with her smile. Even the way she walked seemed wrong.

She handed him a beer, checked whatever it was that bubbled away on the stove, then returned to the table to sit opposite him. 'So, tell me all about it. Did Emmy recognise Lucas from his photograph?'

Was that it? Was she just worried about Harry and Emmy and their futures? He needed to check. 'Is everything okay here?'

'Yes, of course.'

He still didn't get that smile.

'Well?' She raised an eyebrow.

'Yes, Emmy identified Lucas as Harry's father.'

She leant forward. 'And?'

'And she read your letter. That seemed to clinch it. Whatever else you think, she trusts your judgement, Sapphie. She's agreed to let me adopt Harry.'

'Oh, I'm so glad!'

She sat back with a smile—a real smile—and that was when it hit him. Those earlier smiles—they'd been fakes. Until tonight, he couldn't recall Sapphie ever giving a false smile. Not once.

'The lawyers are onto it as we speak. I need to be assessed by Social Services, and then there's a twenty-eight-day waiting period after Emmy signs the consent form, but...' He shrugged. 'Nobody seems to envisage any problems.'

'That's wonderful.'

Her lips still curved upwards, but the reserve had crept back into her face. He worked at keeping his voice even. 'You want to tell me what's wrong?' He could add wariness to that mix now too, he noted.

She jumped up to check the pot on the stove. Again. 'There's nothing wrong.'

He had no intention of playing games or pussyfooting around. 'Are you regretting that we became lovers?'

She stiffened. 'Of course not!' But she didn't turn around.

'I'm not sure what other conclusion I can come to. At the moment you don't exactly seem thrilled to see me.'

She replaced the lid on the pot, set the spoon down, and then she turned. She slid her hands into the back pockets of her jeans. 'That's not the impression I meant to give.'

She stayed where she was. He wished she'd come and sit at the table again, where he could reach across and touch her if he needed to.

His chest tightened. Perhaps that was why she stayed where she was.

She swallowed. 'Liam, I've enjoyed our lovemaking.' One shoulder lifted. 'I think that's been fairly obvious. And I know I said no promises, and that we'd just live in the moment, but…'

Her gaze slid away. He went hot all over. Then cold. He wanted to shove back his chair, push out through the door and storm off into the gathering dusk—because, selfish as he was, he knew he didn't want to hear what she was about to say.

He tried to swallow, but his mouth had gone too dry. He knew what she wanted. She wanted some sign, some proof of commitment from him. He couldn't give it to her. Oh, he doubted she'd mention marriage—at least not yet. But it would be on her mind. His body started to ache as the walls of the trap threatened to close its jaws around him and crush him, suffocate him.

He'd been an idiot, and this served him right. It was what happened when a guy ignored the for ever in a woman's eyes and simply lived in the moment. He deserved what was about to come. He deserved every recrimination she would hurl at him. But her tears…

She didn't deserve this. He'd hurt her. She'd made a miscalculation about her feelings and he'd taken advantage of her vulnerability. He should be flogged. Sapphie's eyes weren't made for crying. They were made for laughing and dancing. He closed his eyes and dragged a hand down his face. He couldn't lie to her. He'd let her down as gently as he could, but…

'Liam?'

He opened his eyes and met her gaze.

'I didn't know that making love with someone could create such a…an emotional bond with them.'

This was going to be worse than he'd thought. His throat grew so arid he doubted he could speak even if he wanted to.

For a moment she looked so miserable he wanted to go to her and draw her into his arms, rest her head in the crook of his shoulder and tell her everything would be all right.

Only he couldn't. Because that was a lie.

'I only realised that today, and I don't know if it's a girl thing or not. So…'

She pulled in a breath. Liam held his.

'It's time for us to stop.'

He blinked.

'If we keep going the way we have been I'm going to want more than you're prepared to give. We both know you don't want to remarry. And we both know I have my own life in Perth. We need to stop while we still can. I figure it's possible for lovers to go back to being friends. I hope so, because that's what we need to do. That way I don't get hurt, and you don't feel trapped.'

She was giving him the brush-off!

She stared at him. She lifted her arms. 'Well?'

Well, what?

'Agreed?'

'If that's what you want,' he snapped.

'Of course it is.' She dusted her hands off on her jeans, as if that was a particularly onerous task out of the way. 'I best go check on Harry. He should be awake by now. Dinner will be ready in about an hour.'

'What happens now?' he burst out.

She turned in the doorway. 'What do you mean?'

'Are you still staying for the next fortnight?'

'Of course I am. It's what we agreed, isn't it? You'll start taking over more of Harry's care while I step into the background. I still think that's what's best for Harry, don't you?'

'Yes.'

'Good.' She started to turn away again.

'And then what? You leave and go back to your life in Perth?'

'That was always the plan, Liam.'

With that, she disappeared. Liam stared after her and willed the relief to hit him. He waited...and waited. It suddenly occurred to him that this scenario—Sapphie leaving— was just as bad as the one he'd imagined, the one where she told him she wanted him to marry her.

And he didn't know what that meant.

Alone in bed that night, Liam stared up at the ceiling and tried to make sense of it all. He didn't toss and turn, or shift restlessly against the cool cotton of the sheets, even though his body burned with its need for Sapphie. He stared up at the ceiling and replayed in his mind his every encounter with her—starting from the moment she'd jumped down from the mail plane, ending with their awkward and stilted dinner this evening.

Whichever way he looked at it, he didn't want Sapphie to leave. He didn't want her returning to that perfect life of hers in Perth.

In the darkness his jaw clenched. She could build a perfect life *here*, couldn't she? She wasn't one of those flighty city girls who needed shopping malls, beauty parlours and coffee shops on their front doorstep. She loved to ride. She loved the land. He could tell from the glow in her eyes whenever she surveyed the landscape, from the way she drew the air into her lungs.

She loved Harry.

And Harry loved her.

She could make Newarra her home, couldn't she? She could live and work here with him and Harry as…as part of the family. He'd stick to her friends-not-lovers dictate. It would kill him, but he'd stand by it because he couldn't offer her marriage. He wasn't opening himself up to that again.

But…

She loved Harry. Harry loved her. She had as much right to raise Harry as he did. Her staying was the perfect solution.

Something about the way Liam looked at her when she set a plate of sausages and eggs in front of him for breakfast the next morning made Sapphie's toes curl.

'What are your plans for today?' he asked.

She busied herself making toast soldiers for Harry. 'The usual, I guess. Harry and I have to bake some bread.' She gestured to the pans of dough resting on the bench. 'Perhaps whiz through this end of the house with the vacuum cleaner…maybe potter in the veggie garden for a bit. What about you?'

'Need to finish the repairs on the cattleyards if we're to start mustering in earnest next week.'

She let out a breath, along with some of the tension that had her coiled up tight. The conversation might be inane, but at least it wasn't as stiff and uncomfortable as it had been last night during dinner.

'Sapphie, do you find it boring out here?'

'Boring? What? On Newarra?' She snorted. 'You're joking, right? There's always something to do, and it's different every day. I'll tell you what boring is—it's working in the same office day after day, clocking in and clocking out at the same time, spending eight hours or more staring at a computer screen. Out here you get fresh air and room to breathe. You get a chance to watch the way the light changes the landscape and see how the colours—'

She broke off, suddenly self-conscious.

He stared at her for a moment. 'Is that what you do when you're living in Perth—work in an office?'

'No way!' She buttered a piece of toast and bit into it. 'I'd go crazy. I have three different part-time jobs. I get to meet lots of different people and I'm never bored.'

'That sounds…all right.'

'It is.' It would be even better if all her part-time jobs paid as much as one full-time job and came with the same benefits. She frowned. 'Why are you asking?'

'More interesting than talking cattle prices,' he mumbled, finishing the last of his breakfast. 'Time I got to work.' He paused by the back door, jammed his hat on his head. 'You want to go on a picnic today?'

She swung around in panic. 'No!' No more picnics. No more swimming in waterholes. No more making love!

A slow grin spread across his face, filling her with heat. She had to turn away from the knowing glint in his eyes.

'I'll see you at lunchtime, then.'

'Yep.' The word emerged from her tight and hard. The back door swung shut, jarring her nerves. She pushed another toast soldier towards Harry and scowled at the table. 'A girl ought to be suspicious when a cattleman says that anything is more interesting than beef prices, Harry. *Real* suspicious.'

She placed the few dirty plates into the dishwasher, then dragged one of the pans of bread dough towards her and started to punch it down. 'Darn man!' What was he up to?

Punching down the bread helped loosen some of the tension in her back and shoulders. Only after she'd started punching down the second batch did she allow herself to go back over the breakfast conversation. What was Liam up to?

'Oh, dear Lord!' She stopped mid-punch, stumbled across to the table to fall into a chair. He'd asked her if she found it boring out here. Why?

Because he meant to ask her to stay?

No, no…of course not. But when she recalled the look in

his eyes her heart slipped and slammed. She stared across at Harry, and the ache inside her grew so heavy it expanded to fill her entire soul.

She reached out and brushed one finger down his face. 'Oh, Harry, I love you.' She loved them both.

But she couldn't stay.

When Liam returned to the house for lunch, Sapphie and Harry weren't in the kitchen. Or the living room. He stopped, listened, and started to grin as the unmistakable sound of ABBA drifted to him from the direction of the theatre room.

He stood in the doorway of the darkened room and his grin widened. Sapphie and Harry weren't just watching the *Mamma Mia!* DVD he'd brought back from his trip to Kununurra—they were dancing to it.

With gusto.

Sapphie had picked Harry up and was swinging him around until they were both breathless and giggling. Liam longed to join them. It suddenly occurred to him that this— Sapphie and Harry, laughing and full of life—was what he wanted to come home to every day. It made him feel alive.

Harry threw his head back and chortled. As if she couldn't help it Sapphie started to laugh, and then couldn't seem to stop. Eventually she collapsed to the ground, holding Harry close to her chest. Then she leapt back up, set Harry on his feet and, holding his hands, started to twist.

Liam didn't know what gave him away—perhaps he chuckled out loud—but Sapphie swung towards the doorway, and when she saw him for a brief moment her face lit up, making him feel ten feet tall.

'Look, Harry—here's Uncle Liam!'

She turned Harry to face him, and Harry's face lit up too.

Harry let go of Sapphie's hands, held his arms out and took one step, then two, in Liam's direction. Sapphie's jaw dropped. Liam momentarily lost the use of his limbs. Harry plonked down onto his nappy-clad bottom and clapped his hands.

Liam swept him up. 'Way to go, Tiger!'

'Clever boy!' Sapphie moved in close to kiss Harry's cheek, swamping Liam with her scent. She glanced up into his face, her cheeks went pink, and she backed away. 'I'll, umm…go make lunch.'

And she fled.

He and Harry followed at a more leisurely pace.

He didn't speak while she made lunch, and he waited until Harry was happily engrossed in his food before turning to her. 'Sapphie, we need to talk.'

She practically catapulted a sandwich at him. 'There's nothing to talk about.' She swung away to make her own sandwich.

Her eyes narrowed when she turned and found him watching her a moment later. She gripped the plate in front of her like a shield. 'What?'

It would be best to come right out and say it. 'Sapphie, I—'

'No!'

He frowned at the panic that sped across her face. 'What exactly are you saying no to?'

She didn't move from the bench. She didn't set her plate down. 'I'm not going to stay here at Newarra. And I have a feeling that's exactly what you were about to ask me.'

Frustration seized him by the scruff of the neck. 'Why not?' He leapt to his feet. 'You like it here, don't you? And you love Harry! Come on, Sapph—'

'Don't raise your voice in front of Harry.' Her eyes spat green fire. 'You know how it upsets him.'

Liam bit back a very rude word. Harry didn't seem the least perturbed. He leant across to ruffle Harry's hair. 'Hold the fort, Tiger. We won't be long.' Then he reached across and grabbed Sapphie's hand, and pulled her clean outside to the back veranda.

With his hands at her waist, he lifted her up to perch on the veranda railing. His hands moved either side of her—

partly to support her, partly to ensure he had her full attention. Her sandwich slid off the plate she still held, to fall to the garden below. Liam seized the plate and sent it after it.

'What is wrong with making Newarra your home?' he demanded.

She gripped the railing until her knuckles turned white. The pulse at the base of her throat fluttered. He ached to lower his mouth to it and touch it with his tongue.

'Sapphie, you love Harry.'

Her entire hands turned white.

'You fit in here. You've made a difference to…*everything*!'

'Please don't,' she whispered. 'Please don't say any more.'

Her eyes filled with tears. Liam wanted to pull her into his arms and comfort her. He wanted to make things right for her—so she'd laugh and dance and sing again. He rubbed his hands up her arms. 'Sweetheart, don't cry.'

She clenched her eyes shut at the endearment. She opened them a moment later. 'Please, Liam, let me down.'

He didn't want to, but he couldn't keep her here against her will. He helped her down from the railing, then took a step back. 'Tell me what's wrong.'

She dragged in a breath. Her hands shook. 'There are things you don't know about me. I'm not who you think I am.'

He smiled at that. 'I know all I need to know about you, Sapphie. I know you're generous and kind, and that you can light up a room with your enthusiasm when you walk into it.'

She pressed her hands to her ears as if to block his words. 'You don't know that I had an abortion!'

The silence that followed seemed to ring in his ears. For three whole heartbeats Liam couldn't move. Her words had doused him in ice. Very carefully, he rolled his neck and shoulders. 'You what?'

'I had an abortion. It was some years ago now…and I'm sorry for it.' She dragged in a shaky breath. 'But, considering how hard you and Belinda tried for children, I think it's the kind of thing you should know about me.' She drew in another breath, more ragged than the last. 'I have a feeling knowing that will change the way you feel about me.'

Her eyes pleaded with him to tell her she was wrong, that he still wanted her to stay. He stepped back, something hard and cold invading his insides. 'Were you advised to have an abortion on medical grounds?'

'No.'

'Did you tell the baby's father? Did you even give him a chance?'

She swallowed and shook her head. 'No.'

On that one whispered word, Liam turned and strode towards the steps. He stopped at the top one, cold and numb...yet behind it all blazed a red-hot fury struggling to burst free. She'd been given the gift of a child and yet she'd...

He forced himself down the steps. He didn't turn around. Sapphie was right about one thing—she wasn't who he'd thought she was.

CHAPTER TWELVE

LIAM didn't return to the house for dinner.

Harry ate. Sapphie didn't.

Liam didn't return to the house to help bath Harry, or to put him to bed. He didn't return to sing Harry a goodnight song.

Sapphie spent the hour after she'd put Harry down pacing the kitchen. Eventually she pushed outside to the veranda and peered out into the darkness of the night which, with a three-quarter moon and more stars than a body could count, wasn't all that dark. Liam didn't emerge from any of the shadows.

She recalled the shock that had whitened his face, the hardness that had entered his eyes and turned his mouth to a grim line, and she had to grip her hands together and close her eyes.

What did you expect?

She opened her eyes, searched the garden and surrounds once more. Nothing. 'Regardless of how much you might hate me, Liam, I hate myself more,' she whispered.

At three a.m., Liam tightened the last of the bolts securing the tractor's radiator in place, tossed the spanner to the nearest bench, and pushed his hands into the small of his back. What next? He turned a slow circle, his eyes searching the furthest reaches of the machinery shed. So far he'd greased and oil-changed the three utes. He'd cleaned tack. And he'd fixed a slow leak in the tractor's radiator. There'd be more chores that needed doing. He just had to find them.

His temples throbbed. His arms ached with fatigue. His body cried out for the oblivion of sleep. But he knew his brain wouldn't give it to him.

You don't know that I had an abortion.

Sapphie's words hit him with the same force now that they had when she'd first uttered them.

A low growl left his throat; he wheeled around. When they'd been teenagers his father had set up a punching bag in here for him and Lachlan. He wondered where it was now. The thought of taking his frustration out in such a physical way suddenly appealed.

An abortion.

Didn't she know how blessed…how lucky…?

He slumped down to an upturned crate and dragged his hands through his hair, remembering with agonising thoroughness the years he and Belinda had spent trying so hard to have children—the clenched-fist hope that had been dashed each month, the growing gut-wrenching realisation that his future might not hold children. And yet Sapphie had blithely rid herself of what he and Belinda would have done anything to attain.

He leapt up, started to pace. She'd lied to him too. She'd let him believe she hadn't been with a man since her rape.

No, she hadn't.

That realisation dawned slowly. She'd told him she hadn't expected to desire a man again. It didn't mean she hadn't tried to.

An abortion, though? He swore. He couldn't make it fit with everything else he knew about her. He'd thought her generous and kind, but now…

She is generous and kind.

But…

But nothing.

She'd... She'd...

He froze, shock and a slow, dawning disgust flooding him. He'd condemned Sapphie without a trial—in an instant and without mercy. He'd thought only of himself—his own shock, his own disappointment, his own judgement. He hadn't considered her circumstances, her frame of mind, or her fears. He hadn't thought about her at all.

She'd had an abortion. It didn't change the fact that she was generous. That she was kind. That she made sacrifices that had his jaw dropping. She'd brought him his nephew. She'd helped him forge a bond with Harry—a strong, lasting bond. She'd forced him to confront issues in his past that he'd buried for too long. She'd made him hope again in a way he hadn't thought possible.

In Harry she'd given him a second chance at life, and then she'd shown him how to overcome his fears and reach out and take that chance. She'd trusted him enough to share her body with him. And what had he done? He'd stormed off.

He hadn't given her a chance to explain. He hadn't given her a chance to do anything. By his actions he'd condemned her, when...when she deserved so much more from him.

She'd made a mistake. One mistake. And he'd turned his back on her. He knew she regretted that abortion because a gut-tearing, the-world-had-come-to-an-end expression had enveloped her face.

And he'd walked away.

He collapsed back down to the crate. She was right—he was letting the badness win. His heart beat hard against the walls of his chest. Was that the kind of example he wanted to set Harry?

Was that the kind of man he'd become?

When Sapphie entered the kitchen the next morning, she found Liam already seated at the kitchen table, with Harry's breakfast things in front of him. The sight pulled her up short. How long had he been sitting there? All night?

He looked tired and strong and alone.

A pulse pounded in her throat. She couldn't seem to move. 'Good morning,' she finally managed.

'Morning.'

She had a feeling he'd left off the 'good' from his greeting deliberately. His face was impassive, unreadable. Beneath it he could be seething with anger or with pain. She couldn't tell.

He stood with that unconscious grace that even now she couldn't help admiring, and came over to take Harry from her. Without a word he gathered up Harry's breakfast things and walked straight out through the back door.

He couldn't have made it plainer if he'd tried—he didn't want Harry anywhere near her. The pain hit her so hard she buckled at the waist, bending over as if someone had landed a punch to her stomach. Liam didn't think her a fit person for Harry to know. He now knew—just as she'd always known— that she had no right being around children.

She limped over to a chair and lowered herself into it.

Liam was right, but even after seven years she found the truth hard to accept. She didn't deserve to have any children. She didn't deserve to have any dealings with children. She deserved *this*. But Liam hadn't even let her kiss Harry goodbye!

'Tears, Sapphie?'

She jumped. Liam stood silhouetted in the back door. She brushed her hands across her face. 'Tears aren't necessarily a bad thing. Considering the losses you've suffered in your life, you'd be a very hard man indeed if you hadn't shed a few yourself.' He didn't say anything, so she forced herself to glance around the kitchen. 'What did you forget?'

'Nothing.'

She frowned. 'Where's Harry?'

'He's having breakfast with Rob today.' He moved into

the room, hooked out a chair and planted himself in it. 'We need to talk without interruptions. And it *is* okay,' he added when she opened her mouth. 'Harry has his toys, and Rob has the know-how.'

She swallowed, then nodded. It was Liam who was adopting Harry, not her. It was Liam's responsibility to decide what was best for him.

'What have you lost, Sapphie, to make you cry?'

'Harry.' *And you*, she added silently, though she couldn't say those words out loud. They hadn't made any promises to each other. Liam had never been hers to lose.

'You are still Harry's aunt. You and Harry love each other and share a bond. I'm not going to stop you seeing him.'

Her breath caught. He wasn't? 'Even knowing what you now know?'

'Tell me about your abortion.'

Exhaustion swept over her. She rested her elbows on the table and her face in her hands. Eventually she pulled them away to find Liam watching her closely. 'What's the point? You already have me tried and condemned.' Rightly so.

Was he really still prepared to let her see Harry?

'I have no right to judge you, Sapphie. I've made mistakes in my life. I'm not perfect. It struck me at about four o'clock this morning that I have no right to expect you to be perfect either.'

Her mouth dropped open. 'But...'

'Yesterday afternoon I was shocked and angry. Angry because all I could think about was what Belinda and I had gone through. Shocked because I couldn't make an abortion fit with everything else I know about you.'

She sensed then the betrayal he'd felt at her revelation.

'I'd like the opportunity to try and understand.'

She avoided talking about her abortion more than she did about the rape. She hadn't told *anyone* about the abortion, but perhaps she owed Liam that much.

'How old were you? Why did you think an abortion was better than another option?'

'I was eighteen.' She had to pause to swallow. 'I was an emotional mess. My mother had just died, and then there was the rape—not to mention the fact that I was in charge of a twelve-year-old girl. I didn't have room in my life for a baby. I mean, it was going to be a struggle to make enough money to support Emmy and me, but a tiny baby that would need around-the-clock care—I didn't know how I'd manage that too.'

She bit her lip, remembering how her fear and panic had driven her decision seven years ago. She'd felt as if some nameless destructive force had backed her into a corner. She hadn't been able to see any way out.

'You were so young,' Liam murmured.

'But that's not even the worst of it.' She forced herself to press on. 'I was so afraid I'd hate the child. That I wouldn't be able to get over the way it had been conceived and—'

Liam reached over to grab her hand. 'You fell pregnant as a result of your *rape*?'

She nodded. 'And you want to know something awful? One of the things that went over and over in my mind was what if the man who raped me sued for custody of the child?' She shook Liam's hand free, to leap up and pace in front of the table. 'A man like that shouldn't be allowed to have custody of a child.'

Liam leapt to his feet too, but she waved a hand at him to tell him to stay where he was.

'That's not even the very worst thing, though.' He might as well know everything. She halted, gripped the back of a chair. 'I couldn't help wondering—what if the child grew up to be a rapist, like its father?' She'd woken at nights in a cold sweat with that thought circling round and round in her head, tormenting her. 'How wicked is that? To project that kind of history and…and hatred onto an innocent child?'

She remembered the darkness, the fear…the locking of herself in the bathroom so Emmy wouldn't see her cry. She remembered the despair that, whichever way she'd turned, had threatened to close over her head and suffocate her. The sickening realisation that if she couldn't even keep herself safe, how could she possibly keep Emmy safe…or anyone else? And for a moment it all threatened to reach out and encompass her again.

'Sapphie?'

Something in Liam's voice hauled her back. He moved around the table to take her shoulders in his hands, to turn her to face him.

'What happened to you, Sapphie, it's…I'm sorry!' His voice was low and fierce. 'I shouldn't have walked away from you yesterday. I should've known better.'

A bubble of hysteria left her lips. 'Don't apologise to me, Liam. I don't deserve it!'

His hands tightened about her shoulders. 'There isn't a soul I know who'd blame you for what you did.'

'Why not?' She pulled free as an unfamiliar anger surged through her. 'I *should* be condemned for what I did. Don't you see? I did what was best for me—not what was best for the child.'

She hadn't deserved that child. *She didn't deserve any children.*

She wheeled away. 'Oh, I was right about one thing. I wasn't the right person to raise it.' She swung back. 'But that doesn't mean someone else wasn't! I should've given birth to the baby and had it adopted by someone who would love it with a whole heart. I should've given the baby its chance.'

She stared at Liam and all her anger drained away, leaving her shaking and limp. She eased back down to her chair, hunched into it, hoping to make herself so small she might disappear altogether.

Liam knelt down in front of her, gripped her hands. 'Sapphie, didn't you get counselling at the time? Didn't one of your friends insist on—?'

'I didn't tell anyone I was pregnant.'

Shock reflected in his eyes. 'Why not?'

'Because I was so ashamed.'

He cupped her face. 'Of what?'

'Of getting myself into a situation where I had been raped. Of trusting a man I thought a friend. Of not being able to bring him to justice so he couldn't do it again. If I'd fought harder… But I couldn't. There was Emmy. But all I achieved was to bring more upheaval and pain into her life anyway.'

The gentleness reflected in his eyes made her tears fall. 'I didn't know how to explain any of it to her. I didn't want to. She'd been through enough.' A sob shook her. 'I just wanted to make all the badness go away. I know I wasn't thinking straight, but at the time I thought having an abortion would make everything go back to how it was before I was raped… But I was wrong. I didn't know it would make me feel so bad. I didn't know I'd regret it for the rest of my life.'

She covered her face with her hands then, and let the sobs overtake her. She didn't have the strength to fight them any more.

With a muffled oath he pulled her against his chest. She'd been right—he'd let the badness win. The man he'd been before Belinda—*that* man would never have walked away from Sapphie yesterday.

Lifting her, he carried her through to the living room and sank down on the sofa. He held her on his lap, stroked her hair and let her sob.

Eighteen, practically alone in the world, and desperately trying to do the right thing by Emmy. He doubted he could have managed it all with half the grace Sapphie had. It would have left him bitter and twisted.

It had left her racked with guilt.

He set his shoulders. He would find some way to help her allay that guilt, to help her move on. Sapphie only ever wanted what was best for others. It was time she stopped punishing herself.

Finally she quietened and her sobs eased. Although she didn't lift her head, he sensed she hadn't fallen asleep. He kept stroking her hair until a strange kind of peace descended over them. Only then did he speak. 'Sapphie, do you really believe the abortion was a mistake?'

She lifted her head. The sadness in her eyes clenched at his heart. 'Yes, I do.'

He traced the curve of her cheek with his finger. 'Don't you think it's time to forgive yourself for that mistake?'

She shook her head. 'It's too big to forgive.'

'No, it's not.' He said the words gently. He moved his finger from her cheek to her lips to prevent all the words he saw trembling there from tumbling out. 'You have a big heart, Sapphie. You give a lot to others. You've done so much for Emmy, for Harry, for me. You've made sacrifices I'm in awe of.'

'None of those things change the fact that what I did was wrong,' she whispered against his finger.

He had to pull it away. The warmth of her breath on his bare flesh was too much to take. 'Maybe,' he agreed, 'but you refuse to take into account your state of mind at the time. You'd just lost your mother. You'd been raped. And you were so young. You had no one to help you. That's a recipe for disaster in anybody's book. And, Sapphie, you seem to have forgotten it wasn't your fault that you fell pregnant in the first place.'

'But—'

'You would never judge a friend—Anna or Lea, for example—as harshly as you've judged yourself.'

Her mouth closed. She frowned.

'Answer me honestly. What would you do if Anna was sitting here telling you this story now? Would you condemn her?'

'No!'

'Then why should you condemn yourself?'

'I don't have the right to judge anyone else. And it's harder to forgive yourself than it is to forgive somebody else.'

'But it's not impossible. You taught me that. I never thought I'd forgive myself for not getting Lucas the help he needed, for not seeing that he needed it.'

She stared at him for a moment. 'But you have?'

He searched inside himself. 'Yes,' he finally said. 'It seems I have.'

Their gazes caught and held. He reached out and pushed a strand of hair out of her face. 'I know these things aren't mended overnight, but promise me you'll think about all I've said. Sapphie, don't let the badness win.'

She blinked. Very slowly, she nodded. 'Okay.'

All of sudden it seemed to hit her where she sat— squarely in his lap. 'Oh!' She scrambled off to sit on the sofa beside him. If he hadn't missed the warm weight of her so much he'd have grinned at the foot of space she'd put between them.

She clenched her hands in her lap. 'Liam, when you were gone last night I came to a decision.'

He stared at her clenched hands and the hairs at his nape stood on end. 'A decision?'

'I've decided to leave on the next mail plane. I think it's for the best.'

'But...' He shot to his feet. 'That's tomorrow!'

'There's no conceivable reason for me to stay here any longer.'

'Harry—'

'Will be just fine. You and he belong together.'

Perspiration gathered beneath his collar, trickled down his back. 'But—'

'It's time I returned to my real life. And, Liam, I want to see Anna and Lea.'

The sheer straightforward simplicity of her argument stole

his breath. He couldn't argue with her wanting to see her half-sisters. But... 'Harry will *always* need you.'

Sadness filtered through the smile she sent him. 'I hope so. But he doesn't need me now as his full-time carer. He has you, and Beattie and Rob, and all your family.'

All his family? Suddenly that didn't seem enough.

CHAPTER THIRTEEN

SAPPHIE said her goodbyes to Harry. She nuzzled her face against Harry's cheek, then blew raspberries against his neck until his laughter filled the air. From the way Rob's eyebrows rose, Liam figured his scowl must have taken over his whole face.

Sapphie handed Harry to Rob, and reached up to kiss Rob's cheek. The young ringer went bright red, and for some reason Liam felt a jolt of jealousy run through him.

'I'll be seeing you, then, Miss Sapphie.'

'Goodbye, Rob. Bye-bye, Harry.'

Harry grinned and opened and closed his hand in his version of a wave. It made Liam's stomach clench. How would he console Harry when the little boy finally realised Sapphie wasn't coming back?

Sapphie dived into the ute Liam had waiting for her. 'Be back soon,' he grunted to Rob, sliding into the driver's seat and gunning the engine.

He glanced across at her as they headed towards the airstrip. Her nose had gone bright red—a sign that told him she was fighting tears. If she cried he'd hold her.

He didn't want her to cry, he didn't want her hurting...but he did want to hold her.

He pulled the ute to a halt by the airstrip. According to the satellite radio, the mail plane would be here some time within the next ten minutes.

Silence, except for the occasional birdcall, filled the car. Liam unclenched his hands from around the steering wheel. 'When will you come and visit?'

'I've been thinking about that. When I come to the Kimberley I want to take Harry to Jarndirri.'

She didn't want to stay at Newarra? Every muscle froze solid. With a superhuman effort he turned his head to look at her. She stared directly out through the windscreen. 'Why?' he croaked.

'I want him to know my family too. I want him surrounded by people who will love him and support him. Do you have a problem with that?'

Yes! Who would fill his homestead with ridiculous pop tunes? Who would make the walls ring with laughter? Who would make caramel milkshakes and crack silly jokes and—?

The sound of Sapphie's car door closing slammed him back to the present. He realised then that the sound filling his ears was the mail plane coming in to land.

Sapphie was leaving.

He shot out of the car, gripped the door for support as he watched her unload her suitcase from the tray of the ute. 'Sapphie, you and Harry belong together as much as Harry and I do. Stay and make your home here. I swear to you we can make it work.'

She lowered her suitcase to the ground. 'Stay here as what?'

His mouth went dry. 'Stay as a part of the extended family. Work and live with us. Make Newarra your home.'

She glanced about at the red dirt and low scrub. His heart thudded against the walls of his chest. *She had to say yes.*

Her gaze returned to his. 'Liam, you've made me believe it's time to stop punishing myself for all the mistakes I've made in my life. You've made me believe my dreams can come true. A week ago I might've said yes to your offer, but now…'

Ice trickled down his back. 'Now?'

'Now I want more. I don't want to be considered part of your extended family. I'm not related to you, Liam.'

She pushed away from the back of the car and moved towards him. His blood fired to life in response to the desire that smoked up her eyes. He should back up, move away... stop her.

'Uh, Sapphie—'

'Liam, I don't feel the least bit related to you. And what I feel certainly isn't platonic.'

She stopped in front of him and ran her hands up his chest to lace her fingers behind his head. Standing on tiptoe, she leant in and touched her lips to his.

He tried to remain impassive, unmoved, but his hands went to her waist. He told himself it was to steady her, only he found he drew her closer. Her lips moved against his more firmly and his fingers curved against her flesh. With a super-human effort he managed not to crush her to him. He did open his mouth to her. He couldn't help it. But he let her maintain the lead and set the pace.

Thick, hot need flooded him as she deepened the kiss, her tongue tangling with his, and overlaying it all was a deep, rich sweetness. It took him over, carried him along as if he drifted on a lazily running river and she was all he needed to stay afloat.

He groaned when she stepped back. She pulled in a breath and met his gaze head on. 'I love you, Liam, and I want it all—you, me and Harry, as a family for ever.'

Fear hit him in the chest, the stomach. He locked his knees against it and backed up a step, tried to shake off the effects of that kiss. He wanted her, but...

A light went out in her brilliant green eyes. 'That's what I figured,' she whispered, reading the answer in his face. 'I'm sorry, Liam. I have to go.'

Sid shuffled up to them. 'I hear the little lady wants to hitch a ride to Broome?'

'You hear right,' Sapphie said. 'And I am nobody's little lady!'

'Right.' Sid straightened. 'I'll, umm, take your bag, then. Oh, and here's Newarra's mail.' He tossed a bag to Liam then caught the one Liam, threw back to him. 'I'll be seeing you.'

'Bye, Sid.' Liam pulled in a breath, then thrust his hand out towards Sapphie. 'Goodbye, Sapphie.'

She ignored the hand. She reached up on tiptoe and kissed his cheek. 'Take care of yourself, Liam.'

She turned and disappeared inside the plane. Liam stumbled to the car, dropped down into the driver's seat, and lifted a hand to touch the spot where Sapphie's lips had rested so briefly. Even now she was more generous than—

The plane's propellers started.

It hit him then. What he had to admit to himself…

And what he had to tell Sapphie.

'All buckled up?' Sid asked.

'Uh-huh.' Sapphie nodded. She couldn't manage anything more. Her throat had practically closed over. Sid taxied to the end of the airstrip, turned the small aircraft around, and though her eyes had started to blur she could see Liam's dusty ute sitting to one side.

The plane's engine revved. Sapphie closed her eyes. She didn't think she could bear to see Liam lift his arm in farewell as they sped past. The plane started to surge forward. She kept her eyes resolutely shut. She didn't want to watch as Newarra faded into the distance.

'What the—?' Sid applied the brakes. Sapphie's eyes flew open.

Liam had driven his ute straight out into the middle of the runway. She planted her hands on the dash in front of her as Sid applied the brakes harder and harder.

'What does he think he's doing?' she squeaked. He could be squashed flat!

'Lost his mind,' Sid grumbled, pulling the plane to a halt, stopping only centimetres from the car. He glanced at Sapphie. 'Over a woman, I'd say.'

She gave a horrid high-pitched laugh. 'You're wrong there, Sid. I happen to know that for a fact as—'

She didn't get any further, because her door was wrenched open and Liam levered himself up to her level. His face was white, his lips were white, but his eyes were blue and blazing.

'Get down from there, Sapphie.'

'I'll do no such—'

He leant in and kissed her. She melted in her seat. His hands found the seatbelt and unbuckled it. She couldn't so much as lift a finger to stop him.

In the next moment she found herself gathered up in his arms, drawn out of the plane and set down on firm ground again.

'Sorry for the delay, Sid, but you can be on your way now.'

She swung around and pointed a finger at Sid. 'Don't you dare!'

'Ain't going nowhere,' he said calmly. 'Not while that ute's in the way.'

She swung back to Liam. 'Have you lost your mind?'

'You can't leave, Sapphie.'

She couldn't keep it together then. She pressed her hands to her cheeks to try and stem the tears.

'Sapphie, don't cry.'

'Please don't do this to me, Liam.' He had to know he was tearing her in two.

'I'm not trying to hurt you.' He touched her shoulders, cupped her face. 'I'm trying to tell you what an idiot I've been. I'm trying to tell you I love you, and that I can't live without you.'

Her jaw dropped.

'I've been pretending I wanted you to stay for Harry's sake. That's a lie. I want you to stay for *me*.'

She stared at him. 'But you just said…'

'The truth didn't hit me till those propellers started up. But when they did it hit me that I loved you. I've spent so long trying to protect my heart that I didn't see what was right in front of my nose—that letting you go would hurt me worst of all.'

The first thread of hope started to trickle through her. 'You really mean it? You really do love me?'

'With my soul and my body…and with my heart,' he vowed.

He strode away from her then, to search the edge of the airstrip. She gaped at him. 'What are you *doing*?' He should be kissing her!

'There's never any darn flowers around when a man needs them,' he muttered. He swung back. 'Hold out your hands,' he ordered.

She cupped her hands in front of her.

Her breath caught when he went down on one knee.

'Sapphie, I can't offer you anything except this land we're standing on…' he picked up a handful of dirt and poured it into her cupped hands '…and myself. I love you. You bring me joy and hope and a happiness I never knew possible. I will dedicate my life to making you happy if you'll agree to marry me and become my wife.'

Her heart all but stopped. She stared at him in openmouthed awe…and then at the dirt in her hands—a mixture of red sand and rock. 'Quick, Liam, get me a container.'

His brow creased. 'I… What?'

She stamped a foot. 'Hurry!'

He leapt to his feet and bolted to the back of the ute. She heard him emptying something metallic out onto its tray, then he swung back with an old instant coffee tin in his hands. Very carefully Sapphie poured the dirt she held in her hands into the tin—every last grain of it, and then she took the lid and sealed it.

She held the tin against her heart and gazed up into Liam's face. 'This is the most precious gift anyone has ever given me,' she whispered. 'I love you, Liam. I would love to marry you. I can't think of a single thing that would make me happier.' A shaft of mischief pierced her. 'Unless, of course...' she leaned in close to whisper '...it's being the mother of your children.' Her smile became a grin. 'Starting with Harry.'

Liam cupped her face in his hands. 'I love you, Sapphire Thomas.'

'I love *you*, Liam Stapleton,' she managed, before his lips descended to hers in a kiss that almost made her weep with its sweetness.

'Uh...' She licked her lips when Liam lifted his head, wriggled against him suggestively. 'Why don't we, umm, go and practise making those babies right now?'

'I'd appreciate it if you'd move the ute first,' Sid said wryly from behind them.

'Oh!' Sapphie swung around, her face red.

Liam slid an arm around her waist and pulled her in close. 'Sure thing, Sid.'

'Congratulations to you both.' Sid grinned and touched the brim of his hat, winked at Sapphie. 'I guess that means you don't need a ride to Broome after all, huh?'

'Umm...no.'

Oh, Broome—Anna and Lea! She swung to Liam. 'Do you think we could fly to Broome later today, and then on to Yarraji? Please? I have to ask Anna and Lea something very important.'

'What's that?'

Her heart filled to nearly bursting. 'If they'll be my brides-maids.'

His grin when it came was slow and sexy. 'We can do whatever you want,' he promised. 'I want you to have it all.'

'I already have it all right here,' she whispered, pulling his head down for another kiss.

They surfaced several long moments later. 'Maybe we'll go visiting tomorrow,' she amended.

'Excellent idea,' Liam agreed, kissing her again.

Sid went back to leaning against his plane. Moving the ute might take a whole lot longer than he'd anticipated. And for once he didn't mind waiting.

EPILOGUE

One month later

'AND this is the colour I've chosen for the bridesmaids' dresses.'

Sapphie pulled a square of golden-brown silk from the bag at her feet. The light filtering in at the French doors caught the shimmering magic of the fabric. She was to be married from Jarndirri in one month's time. With Anna and Lea as her bridesmaids. She could hardly wait!

She shot Lea a grin. 'Can you live with this?'

She'd teased Lea the previous day, not long after Anna and Lea had arrived at Newarra. She'd told her she'd chosen a pink taffeta with a purple appliqué for the bridesmaids' dresses. The expression on Lea's face had been priceless. She and Anna had rolled around the bedroom floor laughing while Lea had feigned affront. But they'd known she'd been having as much fun as them.

Sapphie still found it…*wonderful*…how welcoming, how overjoyed Anna and Lea had been, when she'd told them she was their half-sister. She'd told them everything. The bond between them had gelled and set so hard she knew that nothing earthly could break it.

Lea took the square of silk, stroked it. 'It's lovely.' For a moment longing stretched across her face, and Sapphie wanted to hug her. Only she knew Lea wouldn't appreciate such an overt sign of emotion.

Lea handed the swatch back. 'I'm glad the truth finally came out, Sapphie.'

'Me too,' Anna said softly.

'Me three.' Sapphie grinned, feeling unaccountably blessed.

Lea's face darkened. 'It should've come out sooner. Dad was—'

'Human,' Sapphie jumped in, when she saw Anna's smile start to slip. 'He loved your mother so much he couldn't bear to taint her memory. I...I must've been a symbol to him of all the ways he felt he'd failed her.'

From what Sapphie could figure out, in despair over his wife's failing health, Bryce had turned to Dana for comfort. A fleeting comfort that had left him racked with guilt.

'And don't forget he never shunned me. He never sent Dana away. Like all of us, he made mistakes. And he died before he could make amends.' She paused again. 'Really, all he wanted to do was preserve your mother's memory.'

'Loving like that,' Lea said shortly, 'it's dangerous.'

Sapphie and Anna exchanged a glance, but neither one of them spoke. Then they shared a secret smile. One day some man would sweep Lea off her feet, and then she'd know. Sapphie prayed it would happen soon. She wanted both her sisters as deliriously happy as she was.

Anna leant forward to clasp Sapphie's hand. 'You've made your peace with him, then?'

'Yes, I have.' Life was too short to hold grudges.

A month ago—when she'd gone to Anna and Lea with the truth—Jared had shown her Bryce's will, and he'd given her a letter Bryce had left for her. 'He hoped you'd never have to get this letter, Sapphie. He expected to be here in person to explain, to try and make amends.' He'd left her then to read it.

Bryce had left her a bequest—she'd inherited a bloodline. Jarndirri was famed for its breeding stock. The profits from every animal born through Jarndirri's prestigious Phoenix line now came to her. It was a steady and generous source of income, but Sapphie knew it was more than that. Bryce had found a way to link her to the land he'd worked and loved. It told her in a way that nothing else could that he'd loved her and valued her. It told her he'd meant it when he'd said in his letter *Sapphie, please forgive me.*

'And Emmy?' Anna asked.

Sapphie's heart clenched for a moment. It always ached whenever she thought about her little sister. 'She's started on a drug rehabilitation programme, and she's decided to do some studying, get some qualifications. I'm keeping my fingers crossed for her.'

Anna squeezed her hand. Lea leant forward. 'Tell her we're here if she needs us. Any time.'

Sapphie had to blink back tears. 'Thank you.' She paused and swallowed. 'Emmy told me the reason she didn't ask me to adopt Harry was because she didn't want to ruin my life a second time. Can you believe that? But we had a good talk. I'm looking forward to spending some time with her when she's released.'

Anna and Lea both smiled. 'Good!' they said at the same time.

'Hello, ladies, I thought you might like refreshments.'

Sapphie swung to stare at Liam as he entered the room, bearing a tray. He had Harry tucked under his free arm. Sapphie's heart skipped and danced at the sight of him.

He grinned. 'And someone wanted to visit.'

Anna jumped up immediately to take Harry. 'Hello, gorgeous boy!'

Harry waved his arms and grinned back at her. Sapphie held her breath, but no sadness shadowed Anna's face. Anna radiated that contented, deep-rooted glow of a woman who knew she was loved. Sapphie was glad of it.

And then Anna started to laugh when she saw what was on the tray. 'Caramel milkshakes!'

'Nothing but the best for my future sisters-in-law.' Liam grinned, setting the tray down. 'And nothing but the best for my beautiful future wife,' he murmured in Sapphie's ear.

His lips descended to hers, and she kissed him back with her whole heart.

* * * * *

Harlequin offers a romance for every mood!
See below for a sneak peek from our suspense romance line
Silhouette® Romantic Suspense.
Introducing HER HERO IN HIDING by
New York Times *bestselling author Rachel Lee.*

Kay Young returned to woozy consciousness to find that she was lying on a soft sofa beneath a heap of quilts near a cheerfully burning fire. When she tried to move, however, everything hurt, and she groaned.

At once she heard a sound, then a stranger with a hard, harsh face was squatting beside her. "Shh," he said softly. "You're safe here. I promise."

"I have to go," she said weakly, struggling against pain. "He'll find me. He can't find me."

"Easy, lady," he said quietly. "You're hurt. No one's going to find you here."

"He will," she said desperately, terror clutching at her insides. "He always finds me!"

"Easy," he said again. "There's a blizzard outside. No one's getting here tonight, not even the doctor. I know, because I tried."

"Doctor? I don't need a doctor! I've got to get away."

"There's nowhere to go tonight," he said levelly. "And if I thought you could stand, I'd take you to a window and show you."

But even as she tried once more to pull away the quilts, she remembered something else: this man had been gentle when he'd found her beside the road, even when she had kicked and clawed. He hadn't hurt her.

Terror receded just a bit. She looked at him and detected signs of true concern there.

The terror eased another notch and she let her head sag on the pillow. "He always finds me," she whispered.

"Not here. Not tonight. That much I can guarantee."

*Will Kay's mysterious rescuer protect her
from her worst fears?
Find out in HER HERO IN HIDING
by New York Times bestselling author Rachel Lee.
Available June 2010,
only from Silhouette® Romantic Suspense.*

Four friends, four dream weddings!

On a girly weekend in Las Vegas, best friends Alex, Molly, Serena and Jayne are supposed to just have fun and forget men, but they end up meeting their perfect matches! Will the love they find in Vegas stay in Vegas?

Find out in this sassy, fun and wildly romantic miniseries all about love and friendship!

═══════════════════════

Saving Cinderella! by MYRNA MACKENZIE
Available June

Vegas Pregnancy Surprise by SHIRLEY JUMP
Available July

Inconveniently Wed! by JACKIE BRAUN
Available August

Wedding Date with the Best Man
by MELISSA MCCLONE
Available September

Silhouette *Desire*

From *USA TODAY* bestselling author

LEANNE BANKS

CEO'S EXPECTANT SECRETARY

Elle Linton is hiding more than just her affair with her boss Brock Maddox. And she's terrifed that if their secret turns public her mother's life may be put at risk. When she unexpectedly becomes pregnant she's forced to make a decision. Will she be able to save her relationship and her mother's life?

Available June
wherever books are sold.

Always Powerful, Passionate and Provocative.

SD73031

HARLEQUIN® *Blaze*™

is proud to present

New York Times bestselling author

Vicki Lewis Thompson

with a brand-new trilogy,
SONS OF CHANCE
**where three sexy brothers
meet three irresistible women.**

Look for the first book
WANTED!

*Available beginning in June 2010
wherever books are sold.*

red-hot reads

www.eHarlequin.com

HB79548

LARGER-PRINT BOOKS!

GET 2 FREE LARGER-PRINT NOVELS PLUS
2 FREE GIFTS!

HARLEQUIN® Romance®

From the Heart, For the Heart

YES! Please send me 2 FREE LARGER-PRINT Harlequin® Romance novels and my 2 FREE gifts (gifts are worth about $10). After receiving them, if I don't wish to receive any more books, I can return the shipping statement marked "cancel." If I don't cancel, I will receive 6 brand-new novels every month and be billed just $4.07 per book in the U.S. or $4.47 per book in Canada. That's a saving of at least 22% off the cover price! It's quite a bargain! Shipping and handling is just 50¢ per book.* I understand that accepting the 2 free books and gifts places me under no obligation to buy anything. I can always return a shipment and cancel at any time. Even if I never buy another book from Harlequin, the two free books and gifts are mine to keep forever.

186/386 HDN E5N4

Name	(PLEASE PRINT)	
Address		Apt. #
City	State/Prov.	Zip/Postal Code

Signature (if under 18, a parent or guardian must sign)

Mail to the **Harlequin Reader Service:**
IN U.S.A.: P.O. Box 1867, Buffalo, NY 14240-1867
IN CANADA: P.O. Box 609, Fort Erie, Ontario L2A 5X3

Not valid for current subscribers to Harlequin Romance Larger-Print books.

Are you a current subscriber to Harlequin Romance books and want to receive the larger-print edition? Call 1-800-873-8635 today!

---

* Terms and prices subject to change without notice. Prices do not include applicable taxes. N.Y. residents add applicable sales tax. Canadian residents will be charged applicable provincial taxes and GST. Offer not valid in Quebec. This offer is limited to one order per household. All orders subject to approval. Credit or debit balances in a customer's account(s) may be offset by any other outstanding balance owed by or to the customer. Please allow 4 to 6 weeks for delivery. Offer available while quantities last.

Your Privacy: Harlequin Books is committed to protecting your privacy. Our Privacy Policy is available online at www.eHarlequin.com or upon request from the Reader Service. From time to time we make our lists of customers available to reputable third parties who may have a product or service of interest to you. If you would prefer we not share your name and address, please check here. ☐

Help us get it right—We strive for accurate, respectful and relevant communications. To clarify or modify your communication preferences, visit us at www.ReaderService.com/consumerchoice.

HRLP10R

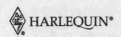

HARLEQUIN®

Showcase

On sale May 11, 2010

Reader favorites from the most talented voices in romance

Save $1.00 on the purchase of 1 or more Harlequin® Showcase books.

SAVE $1.00 on the purchase of 1 or more Harlequin® Showcase books.

Coupon expires Oct 31, 2010. Redeemable at participating retail outlets. Limit one coupon per purchase. Valid in the U.S.A. and Canada only.

52609015

5 65373 00076 2   (8100)0 11651

Coming Next Month

Available June 8, 2010